Murder on the Airship Arcadia

by

Francis J Coyle

Chapter One

Bullet wounds do not heal very fast. My left leg ached, a souvenir from my last case, as I trailed after my cousin, Lady Imogen LaRue. The Airship Arcadia cast a long shadow across the grass, already weathered by the long, hot summer and now trampled underfoot by the steady stream of passengers queueing to board the airship. I could smell ozone in the air, promising a storm.

I carried a single valise. Imogen insisted that I allow the stewards to take my trunk and, for once, I was grateful for the privileges her class and wealth brought. I stepped forward again as the queue moved.

"Where is that dratted girl?" Imogen asked. She peered behind me.

"I am sure she will join us presently." I said.

I shuffled forward again. Ahead I could see the captain of the airship was exchanging pleasantries with a number of passengers. The passengers, I noted, were drinking wine from delicate glass flutes.

"She is always late." Imogen said. "I never should have agreed to bring her on this trip."

I caught the eye of a steward and mimed drinking from a glass. He smiled and brought a tray, offering us drinks. I accepted one for myself and, after placing my valise on the ground, took another for Imogen. The steward bowed and turned to serve another passenger as I sampled the wine. Fruity with a hint of something.

"You know you love her really."

"There she is. Silly girl."

I turned to see Elizabeth Murphy, my second cousin once removed, waving gaily as she ran across the field. I shook my head in amusement as she darted around one of our fellow passengers, nearly bowling him over. She shouted her apologies but continued on.

"Sorry I'm late, auntie. I had such a frightful time with the cab." Elisabeth said. "I'm so excited. This will be my first trip abroad. I'm so looking forward to it. I could not sleep last night waiting for today to start. The porter at the hotel had to call a cab to bring me here."

She twisted a small handkerchief in her hand.

"It is good to see you." I said when she paused for breath. "The last time I saw you, you had pigtails in your hair and you were hiding behind your mother's skirts."

She gave me an enthusiastic hug, almost spilling the drinks.

"Oh, sorry." She said, and gave Imogen a hug.

The queue stepped forward again. I handed Imogen her drink and bent to pick up my valise. Elisabeth was quicker and picked it up for me.

"Thank you."

As I listened to Elisabeth chattering about school and how excited she was to be going on holiday, I took the moment to study the other passengers. The couple in front of me introduced themselves to the captain as Mr and Mrs Potts. Mr Potts was a tall, elderly gentleman dressed in tweed. His hair was silver and he still held himself quite proudly, I thought. Mrs Potts had a kind face. I could see a spark of humour in her eyes when she smiled.

The captain was dressed in the same white suit that ship captains wore. The only indication he was an airship captain was the flight goggles wrapped around his peaked hat.

"I'm afraid our son will not be able to join us on this trip." Mr Potts said.

"I am sorry to hear that." The captain said. "Let us hope that he will join us on a later occasion."

"What did he say?" Mrs Potts asked.

"We're talking about George not coming." Mr Potts replied in a loud voice.

"George?" Mrs Potts said. "Oh no. He is scared at the thought of flying you see. Just gives him the shivers."

I smiled inwardly at the thought. The only reason that I had agreed to join my cousins on this trip was the opportunity to fly. The chance to soar above the clouds and escape my problems for a while. Airships were unmatched in speed and comfort compared to the modern cruise ship. They were also more expensive, so I was grateful to my cousin Imogen for that as well.

Elisabeth was looking at me expectantly.

"Yes, I agree." I blurted.

"You didn't hear a word I said." Elisabeth accused.

I was saved from answering as the queue moved forward again and I was face-to-face with the captain. There was a faint sweet smell from him which I will forever associate with flying.

"May I present Lady Imogen LaRue and Miss Elisabeth Murphy." I nodded towards each of my companions in turn as I introduced them. "I am Ignatius Brown."

"Ahh, the famous Detective Sergeant." The captain said. "You are doubly welcome on-board. We have all read your exploits in the London Standard over the last few weeks. I am Captain Harvey."

I half listened as he briefly described the events of the next few days of travelling. Instead I studied the airship.

At several hundred feet long it was the largest in the world, capable of transporting up to fifty tons of cargo or passengers. The steel ridges, which gave the airship its rigid shape, were covered by thin canvas. They pressed against the skin like the ribs of an emaciated cow. A passenger car towered above me, hanging from the silver cigar shaped balloon. It was slightly forward of the middle of the airship. To the rear of the airship there was a second car.

The captain followed my line of sight.

"That is the steam engine." The captain said. "It is a modern condenser steam engine, which means that we do not need to carry any extra water. As well as powering the propellers to drive us forward, the hot air from the boiler is funnelled upwards into the airship to provide lift to the helium bags."

I nodded knowledgeably. One day, I promised myself, I would make an effort and learn about these new steam engines. It was a man thing. But not today.

"How soon will we arrive at Istanbul?" Elisabeth asked.

"We will be leaving London within the hour. There is a storm approaching so the first stage of our journey to Paris may be delayed but we will catch up. We will arrive in Istanbul on Sunday morning."

"Will it be dangerous, flying in the storm?" Imogen asked.

"Oh, Auntie." Elisabeth said. "Flying is not dangerous. There are no rocks to crash into. We will be perfectly safe."

"When people talk about the dangers of flying, they are thinking of the heavier-than-air biplanes." The captain's voice was very soothing. "Think of the airship as a stately old lady. We will take our time and fly at a sedate pace. If there are any problems, such as bad weather, we will simply tie up for a couple of hours and wait out the storm."

The captain excused himself and introduced himself to the next passengers. I returned my glass to a handy tray and reclaimed my valise from Elisabeth. I could have closed my eyes and still been able to tell the difference between the footsteps of the two ladies as they preceded me up the wide gangplank. Elisabeth darted forward, her light footsteps reverberated on the wooden gangplank. Imogen followed slowly, a stately old lady marching ponderously forward.

I was halfway up the gangplank when I made my first mistake of the voyage. I slipped. I could blame my left leg, the ache was abominable, or perhaps the glass of wine I had drunk but the truth is I was simply clumsy. I tripped over my own feet. My valise crashed to the ground and burst open. A book I was reading slipped free. A letter I had promised to post fluttered to freedom. My old trusty revolver, worn blue from overuse, escaped and clattered down the gangplank to land at the captain's feet.

I grabbed my book and re-clasped the valise. All eyes were watching me as the captain mounted the gangplank and returned the revolver to me. His face was expressionless as I grasped the warm walnut handle of the revolver like an old friend. I smiled weakly at my audience then slipped the weapon into my valise and mounted the gangplank.

Imogen and Elisabeth were waiting for me on the promenade deck.

"I trust there is a good reason for you bringing that onboard." Imogen said.

I was surprised at the coldness of her tone. I know that she did not approve of me carrying a weapon but she knew the dangers I had faced over the last several weeks. I no longer woke screaming at the night terrors. The intense fears I had faced had faded, but there was still evil in the world, and I refused to face it unarmed.

"I may be on holiday," I said, "but I am still a Scotland Yard detective."

"I would like to learn how to shoot someday." Elisabeth said.

"Elisabeth. Come along at once."

I grinned at Elisabeth. She had managed to defuse the situation and at the same time shock her aunt.

"Perhaps you should join the suffragettes." I teased. "They will certainly welcome such a defender."

I followed the two ladies across the open deck. The airship balloon swayed above me in the gentle breeze. Several deck chairs littered the deck, one of which was occupied by an attractive young lady. I tipped my hat towards her and was rewarded with a dazzling smile.

A pair of stewards stood guard at the promenade entrance to the airship. Hat in hand, I followed the taller of the two through a comfortable sitting room, past the doors to a smoking lounge and a dining room, then down a short flight of stairs to the bedroom wing. A long corridor stretched in front of me, with several stateroom doors at each side and at the end. Elisabeth's name adorned the second door on the left. The steward opened it and confirmed to her that tea would be served in the promenade deck in half an hour. My room was next. Then Imogen's.

My trunk had been delivered by the stewards earlier and was on the floor next to a low bed. The mattress was thin, supported by a lattice of wire. I tested it and was pleasantly surprised that it was comfortable. Next to the bed was a small chair. The room was lit by a round porthole on the bulkhead. The walls were made of canvas with a second layer of gaily patterned silk wall-covering. Rather than a wardrobe I had a thin rail with hangers, and a patterned silk curtain as a wardrobe door. The rattan chair squeaked as I sat on it and slowly unpacked my trunk. I hung my suit in the wardrobe, the dinner jacket joined it. My tweed jacket would be sufficient for tea, I decided.

My book, the Biography of Dr John H. Watson, demanded my attention and I returned to the rattan chair to enjoy a leisurely moment of reading. I knew the ladies would take a few moments to wash the travel from their faces so I relished a brief respite from my duty as chaperone.

I was engrossed in the revelations about the wars in India when a discreet knock interrupted my concentration. I unlatched the door to find my cousin Elisabeth looking radiant in a bright green velvet dress. Her red hair was tied up with a black velvet band.

"It is only tea." I said. "An opportunity for passengers to introduce ourselves before the voyage begins."

I know that I'm not supposed to comment on a lady's appearance so I held my tongue for once. I was surprised she had changed.

"Ignatius." Elisabeth paused awkwardly for a moment, then she continued in a rush of words. "I heard about your younger brother Augustus. I don't know how to say how sorry I am."

I did not answer. How can you answer when life punches you in the stomach. The events of the last few weeks flashed across my eyes. Elisabeth must have seen my rage at the unfairness of life because she stepped back. It took a moment to swallow my anger.

Imogen joined us at that moment.

"That just will not do young lady." Imogen said. "If you change your clothes at every moment, you will run out of clothes before we reach Paris."

"But, Auntie."

Imogen tapped her foot imperiously and Elisabeth returned to her room to change.

I am sometimes surprised that the British government had not utilised my cousin Imogen as their secret weapon. The Boer war would not have lasted quite so long if they had placed her, with her tapping foot and expressionless face, on the front lines. It would certainly give me pause if I had to attack such a battleaxe. I am being unfair, of course.

"How's this?" Elisabeth asked.

She had changed back into her original skirt and skirt-waist. Her hair was still tied back, exposing a long neck.

Imogen nodded approvingly and tucked a stray hair back from the young girl's face.

"Let us face the crowd together." Imogen said. She turned and led the way along the corridor towards the promenade deck.

I followed after, the feeling of dread growing in the pit of my stomach.

Chapter Two

A steward sat station at the entrance to the bedroom wing. He stood as the ladies approached and opened the door politely for them. I nodded to him as he resumed his seat, and followed the ladies up the stairs and along the corridor to the promenade deck.

It was as bad as I feared.

I am an introvert. I find any social engagement draining, which surprises many of my friends. As a police detective I am often called to the scene of a crime. This usually involves a large crowd. I find it easy to engross myself in my work, ignore the stares of the curious, and investigate the crime. My friends expect that I am equally able to engage with a crowd in a social scene and they cannot understand why I shy away.

I paused for a moment at the entrance to the promenade deck. There were perhaps a dozen people drinking tea from delicate china cups.

"Pardon me," said a voice behind me. I apologised and stepped to the side.

A gentleman stepped through the door. Silver threads weaved through his dark hair giving him a distinguished appearance to his young face. I guessed he was perhaps in his mid thirties. His clothes were slightly wrinkled but very finely cut. A pair of gold framed spectacles adorned his face.

"I do so love these trips." The young man said. "It will be so wonderful to see Rome again."

His wife joined him at the entrance. She was quite petite with an elfin face. He introduced himself as Horace Vellance and his wife as Penelope Vellance. I introduced myself. I was unsurprised to see the flicker of recognition in his eyes.

"Are you here to solve a murder mystery, detective?" Horace Vellance asked.

I bit off my usual curt reply. I'm on holiday for goodness sake. Can't a detective go on holiday without finding a murder? Instead I laughed as if no one had asked me this question before.

"Perhaps the mystery is why I find myself here." I replied. "My doctor suggested that I take a holiday while I recover and my cousin kindly invited me to join her."

"I certainly hope that your recovery goes well." Horace Vellance said. He nodded to me pleasantly and led his wife to a small table.

"Those two are not what they seem," a voice at my shoulder said.

I looked down and saw the serious face of Elisabeth Murphy looking back at me.

"Why do you say that?" I asked, as she led me to join Imogen at a nearby table. The table was situated slightly back from the centre of the deck where other people were congregating. Perfect for watching other passengers walk past without engaging with them.

"Wasn't it obvious?" Elisabeth asked. "He preceded her through the door and then, when he reached for her hand, she swatted the hand away."

"You should be a detective." I teased. "Detective Sergeant Murphy to the rescue."

A steward handed me a cup of tea in a delicate white cup. I savoured the taste of tea for a moment before swallowing the drink.

"The empire was built on the back of cups of tea like this." Imogen said. I nodded politely in agreement.

There was a moment of quiet as the captain entered the promenade deck. He raised his hands for everyone's attention. "My apologies.

There will be a slight delay to the departure as we are still waiting our last passenger." The bustle of conversation resumed. I heard the word 'disgrace' from a couple of conversations nearby.

"I do not think people are happy with this update." I remarked dryly.

"Look at them," Elisabeth pointed to a couple standing near the promenade entrance, "they seem very upset by this."

"Elisabeth." Imogen said. "It's rude to point. What must they think of us?"

I looked at the couple. The man was wearing a dark charcoal suit with the waistcoat neatly buttoned. I couldn't see his wife behind him, just her hair was visible, elegantly balanced on her head. He had a worried expression on his face.

"From how he's dressed I would say he's a funeral director. Perhaps he's going to be late for a funeral." I said. "Or perhaps he's a banker. Do you notice how his jacket is tucked at his waist?"

"Yes, why?"

"At a guess, he is carrying a hip flask." I said. "Either gin, or more likely whiskey. Ahh, there he goes."

As we watched, the man surreptitiously withdrew a flask from his waist pocket and a dram into the teacup he was holding. His wife stepped into view and I had my first glimpse of her. She was the same lady with the dazzling smile whom I had tipped my hat towards when we first entered the airship.

"Oh." Elisabeth said.

I turned towards her.

"She's wearing the same dress I was wearing earlier." Elisabeth said in response to my raised eyebrow.

"You wore it better." Imogen said.

I recognised Mr and Mrs Potts as they entered the promenade deck and, after a brief word with a steward, were guided to a table next to us. I stood politely and introduced myself and my companions.

"Delighted to meet you Mr Brown." Edmund Potts said as we shook hands. His head was tilted to one side as if he was trying to remember where he had heard my name before.

"Are you travelling to Paris, Rome, or all the way to Istanbul?" Victoria Potts asked.

"We are travelling to Istanbul for a few days, then continuing to Egypt." Imogen said. "My niece, Elisabeth, wanted to be an explorer when she was younger and fell in love with Egypt. It's those adventure books she reads."

"I'm sure it will be a delightful experience for her." Edmund Potts said. "We are travelling to Rome. I have a number of business contacts there whom I've never had the opportunity to meet. It's quite thrilling to travel by airship."

"It's better to fly than to sail." Victoria Potts said.

"Yes, dear." Edmund Potts said in a loud voice.

There was a clatter behind us on the gangplank. I turned to see two stewards climbing the gangplank with a large travelling trunk. A large gentleman with a permanent scowl on his face followed them with a valise in his hand. He was smoking a large cigar.

"This appears to be our missing passenger." I said.

I must have said it too loudly because he turned his scowl in my direction for a moment. The captain distracted him and he swept through the promenade double doors towards the bedroom wing. The gangplank was slowly lifted from the ground.

"We appear to be moving." Imogen said.

The sun chased the shadows across the promenade deck as the Airship Arcadia gracefully started to turn. I could hear the distant cough of the steam engines as they started. There was a scream from the steam engine whistle.

"We appear to be moving backwards." Elisabeth said.

"The steam engines will take a few minutes to start pushing us forwards." Edmund Potts said. "It always starts off a little slow like this, then the propeller drives us forward."

"It must be a strong engine to overcome the breeze." I said.

I was interrupted at this moment by a young man who strode over to me with his hand outstretched. He was quite handsome with a roguish smile on his face.

"Sorry to interrupt." He said with a tone that I thought didn't sound sorry at all. "The gentleman I was speaking to mentioned that you were the famous police detective Ignatius Brown and I wanted to come over and shake you by the hand."

I sighed inwardly and stood to shake his outstretched hand. He introduced himself as Roland Ashton. I introduced my companions, and Mr and Mrs Potts. I did notice with some amusement that my cousin Elisabeth had suddenly become very shy.

I glanced over his shoulder to see Horace Vellance smiling broadly.

"Perhaps you can regale us with one of your escapades?" Roland Ashton asked.

"They would not be suitable for the ladies," I said. I refrained from rolling my eyes at his childish tone. "My escapades, as you call them, are not tales of adventures but stories about surviving against hardened criminals."

"Later then. After dinner. In the smoking lounge."

I agreed to this, if only to get rid of him. He thanked me politely and left.

"I knew your name from somewhere." Edmund Potts said. He pushed himself to his feet and shook my hand again. "I don't mean to embarrass you but, a fine job, you did a fine job."

I thanked him, feeling embarrassed. He nodded to me and resumed his seat. He turned to his wife and loudly started a conversation.

This was another reason why I dreaded these social occasions. The inane comments. The requests from young socialites who saw me as the newest celebrity. My employment with Scotland Yard had afforded me the opportunity to solve crimes and stop murderers. I did not join the constabulary for an adventure. Catching real killers was different from the romance of novels where they solved crimes and still managed to woo the daughter of the victim. In real life, it was about chasing shadows through grime and muck. Trying to avoid getting blood on your shoes while helping victims who were sometimes too terrified to talk.

Crime was not an adventure novel.

My thoughts were interrupted by the sounds of an argument. The large man, who had arrived late, entered. He was still smoking his cigar. He brushed aside the offer of tea from a steward, and brusquely demanded a whiskey. Behind him, there was another gentleman with a large moustache. His countenance was of a brutish appearance, the nose broken and piggy eyes. He stared about him suspiciously. The face seemed familiar for some reason.

They resumed the argument that had attracted my attention.

"Mr 'erts, it's not that I don't want to 'elp you, sir." The man with the brutish face said. "It's just, with the money that you're offering, it doesn't really make it worth my while."

"You agreed to one more job, Bakerson. One … more ... job." Herts said. He jabbed his cigar for emphasis. "Either you're in or you're out. But if you're out then that's it. No more jobs from me."

Bakerson. Of course I knew him. I should have recognised that brutish face. Marcus Bakerson. Thirty-two years old. He had been arrested several times on suspicion of gang violence and blackmail. Nothing could be proven, however. It was standard practice to report the whereabouts of such men if we accidentally bumped into them, so I made a mental note to send a telegraph from our next stop, Paris.

Herts noticed me staring and lowered his voice. In fact, everyone was staring but he locked eyes with me. My fame perhaps has preceded me. Herts and Bakerson moved to a corner of the promenade deck and argued in lowered tones.

"They will be a barrel of laughs on this trip." Elisabeth said.

"Elisabeth, sometimes I despair. I cannot take you anywhere." Imogen said. "You are not supposed to listen in on other peoples' conversations. I am sure those gentlemen have something private to discuss."

I was sure they did and would love to have the chance to listen to them. The steward took this moment to announce that dinner would be ready shortly. I trailed after the ladies to return to our rooms to change for dinner.

Little did I know as I took a last look around the crowded deck that, in a few short hours, one of the passengers present would be murdered.

Chapter Three

Dinner was a quiet affair.

Herts and Bakerson continued to argue quietly at a private table. Imogen rapped my knuckles at one point when she saw I was attempting to listen to them instead of paying attention to our conversation. Elisabeth laughed at this. She then received a short lecture about her table manners.

The conversation flowed as fast as the wine.

During dinner I managed to obtain another glass of that delicious, fruity wine. It was French and a dark, purplish red, which is about as far as my wine knowledge goes, but it did tease the palette quite admirably.

After dinner I sat next to the German diplomat Kurt Heiss and his wife Dorothy in the sitting room. They were delightful company and I lost myself in one of their stories about taking their dachshund on safari in East Africa. Kurt had a war wound in his left leg as well, so I empathised with him. He had been wounded in a skirmish when he was younger. It only throbbed when it rained he told me. He predicted a storm.

I had forgotten the time, when I felt a light touch on my arm. I looked up surprised to see a pair of intense blue eyes staring at me. He introduced himself as Simon Charles.

"I am delighted to meet you Detective Sergeant." Simon Charles said. He introduced his wife Edith. Simon Charles was still dressed like a funeral director. His intense blue eyes brightened up a very grey and tired face. His wife still had that dazzling smile, her eyes watchful under a fashionable hat.

"We have read so much about you." Edith Charles said. Her voice was low and melodious.

I smiled pleasantly.

"Please don't believe everything you read in the newspapers." I said. I stood gallantly to shake her hand. There was a hint of steel in her grip. "We are not allowed to report everything to the newspapers and, when the newsmen can't find a story, they create their own exciting adventures."

Simon Charles extracted a gold-plated pocket watch from his breast pocket. I noticed an inscription on it, but I couldn't read it. He looked pointedly at the face of the pocket watch and coughed.

"Lord Vellance mentioned that you had promised to treat us to a discourse on some of your escapades." Simon Charles said.

With a start I glanced at my own pocket watch. It was later than I had thought.

"Would it be possible for me to join you?" Kurt Heiss asked.

I informed him that it would be a pleasure and rose.

"The smoking lounge has been set up." Simon Charles said.

Elisabeth saw us leave the sitting room and caught me by the arm.

"Aunt Imogen says I'm not allowed to listen to your adventures in the smoking lounge." Elisabeth said. "Please say I can come. Please."

I smiled and shook my head.

"Imogen will be sorely disappointed in me if I take you into the lounge." I said.

I followed Kurt Heiss into the smoking lounge. He gave me an encouraging smile before sitting, drawing a pipe from his pocket. The chairs had been placed in a semi-circle. The three rows were filled with men smoking cigars and pipes. I was grateful when the steward turned on a clockwork smoke extractor to clear the air.

Herts and Bakerson sat in the centre seats of the front row. I raised an eyebrow. Normally the criminal element would shy away from any police attention but it appeared that Bakerson was made from sterner stuff.

I leaned against the lectern. It doubled as a pulpit—I could see a small chalice on a shelf hidden at the back. I coughed awkwardly as I surveyed the crowd. The hubbub died away. A couple of gentlemen at the back had already changed into smoking jackets but most were still dressed for dinner.

"My name is Ignatius Brown." I said awkwardly. "I am a Detective Sergeant with Scotland Yard."

I had attended weekly lectures at my club, the Wednesday Night Club, on Bruton Lane. But this was the first time that I had ever given a lecture.

"Most of you will have read of my recent case in the London Standard. Unfortunately I am not allowed to discuss this case until the courts have raised the reporting restrictions. Instead, with your kind permission, I would like to relate another recent case which I successfully resolved."

I paused for a moment. In the silence I could hear the sound of the wind howling outside, the storm had arrived. I could feel a slight shudder through the airframe.

"The Case of the Missing Cat. An inauspicious title I agree, but it did have an inauspicious start. A constable was alerted by a young schoolboy whose cat had entered an abandoned house through a small window but could not escape. The constable tried to assist the boy and, in the process, discovered the body of a middle aged man. He apparently had a heart attack in the bedroom of the abandoned house. The constabulary were going to dismiss this as another heart attack but we decided on an autopsy, as there was no reason for the man to visit the property.

"The coroner confirmed that the man was killed by curare, which is a rare poison from South America. There was a small puncture wound on his arm through which the poison was administered. We initially thought that the victim had been murdered for his purse, which was missing. At this stage we had yet to identify the victim.

"Our breakthrough came when a passing remark by one of the constables brought to our attention that the victim had a deep tan. For the average English gentleman this would only extend to the face and hands, but for this gentleman it extended to his entire body. We realised that he was from the colonies. The police in New Zealand responded to our telegraph to confirm that he was one of their police constables who was working undercover to bring some criminals to justice.

"A New Zealand constable chasing drug smugglers in England and killed by a South American poison. Another clue that we had was the white clay crusted on his shoes. This led us to the docks at Dover where we confronted a South American drug gang and managed to catch his murderers."

I finished the lecture with a flourish.

I was glad to see that several of the gentlemen were nodding in approval. I had always been taught during my investigative work that methodical investigation, following one clue at a time, was the best way to solve a crime. It was like pulling at the thread of an investigation until the whole pattern unravelled and revealed the killer.

A steward appeared at my elbow and placed a small glass of water on the lectern. I thanked him.

Then the questions came.

To say the questions were varied would be an understatement. My audience certainly showed their versatility and I was convinced by the end of the discussion that most of them could have a future career as a detective…or a serial killer. Between them they had devised the best way to fool even an experienced detective such as myself. I was glad to see that neither Bakerson nor Herts took notes.

I was allowed eventually to escape, and I retired to the sitting room.

Elisabeth was upset. I noticed this as I sat down. My cousin Imogen was talking to another lady with silver hair so I surmised that she was not the reason. I smiled kindly at Elisabeth.

"You have finished your talk then?" Elisabeth asked.

"Yes, thank goodness." I replied smiling. When she did not return my smile, I asked simply. "What is wrong?"

Elisabeth glanced to her right then shook her head. I followed her gaze. Roland Ashton was sitting at a table near the door with an attractive young lady. His handsome face was creased in a broad smile as he teased her with a comment. Her laugh was infectious.

Elisabeth averted her gaze. I managed to divert her for a few moments and even managed to obtain a smile from her.

"Ignatius, come here please."

I obediently stood up and joined Imogen as she introduced me to Mrs Colchester. Elisabeth joined us after a few moments of indecision.

"So you are a member of our constabulary, Mr Brown?"

"I am a Detective Sergeant in Scotland Yard." I said.

"I remember when Scotland Yard was actually based in Scotland Yard." Mrs Colchester said. "Such a dreary building it was too. Why did you join the police?"

"I felt I could do my bit for the local community." I said.

"Yes, but why the police?" Mrs Colchester asked. Her eyes sparkled with mischief. "Surely you could have found a more honest way to serve the community?"

I laughed. It was the same question that every police officer asked himself two or perhaps three times a day. Long nights, the dreary rain, bad pay, and the lack of respect from the public for the rule of law, inserted these troubling thoughts in your mind.

I was saved from an answer by a roar of anger behind me. I sprang to my feet, my right hand feeling for the revolver I was not carrying.

Marcus Bakerson and Roland Ashton were standing face to face. Roland was standing in a very protective position over the young lady he had been flirting with earlier.

"Touch her again and I will kill you." Roland said in a low voice.

"I could break you in 'alf, little man." Bakerson said. He leaned forward, his chin jutted out. "'ere you go, take your best shot."

I watched as a couple of stewards intervened between the two men. Bakerson, his face still bright red, was persuaded to leave.

"Horrible man." Elisabeth's voice was low, but I could hear the fear in her voice.

Conversation restarted after Bakerson left the room but it had that sort of fragile quality you hear after someone has made a bawdy joke or a satirical comment. We, of course, started to talk about the weather.

The young lady was looking very pale but she refused the offer of a glass of water from a steward. Roland offered his arm to the young lady and ushered her from the room.

"In my day such indecorous behaviour would have been beyond the pale." Mrs Colchester said. "Someone would have given him a good thrashing."

"The young lady certainly looked distressed." Imogen said.

"Mrs Fabersham is her name." Mrs Colchester said. "A pretty little thing. She is going to Rome to join her husband."

I glanced at the disappearing Roland Ashton who was assisting the elegant Mrs Fabersham towards the bedroom wing. Herts, I noticed, was staring after them. He had a cruel twist to his lips that I naturally did not like.

"I am sure that Mr Ashton will behave the proper gentleman." Imogen said. She had caught my glance after the couple and correctly deduced the direction of my thoughts.

The discussion changed to general topics about the trip. Mrs Colchester, I gathered, was travelling to Africa on the advice of her doctor. Her son had joined the fallen in the war with the Boers and her husband had recently passed away so she was taking advantage of the comforts of airship travel. She also coached Elisabeth on how to knit.

"My late husband would have enjoyed this adventure." Mrs Colchester said.

The electric lights turned on earlier than expected because of the growing darkness outside. The occasional buffeting of the wind reminded us of the rising storm.

I was invited by Kurt Heiss for a last drink in the smoking lounge. It was not a pleasant experience.

Chapter Four

It had been obvious, to even the most ardent Teutonophile, that England and Germany were heading for a confrontation. Ever since the SMS Panther, a modern gunboat, was sent by the German High Command to the Moroccan port of Agadir, English and French colonies reacted with alarm at the unexpected sight of a steamer flying a German flag. Tensions were increasing and it only took a single mistake for a serious international incident to occur.

Such were the discussions in the smoking room.

The comfortable seats had been rearranged by the stewards into a circle and Kurt Heiss and I found ourselves invited to sit and join the ongoing conversation. As the German representative, Kurt Heiss was allowed a few moments to be furnished with a drink from an attending steward, before being questioned by the onlookers.

"I know that it is not your fault." Simon Charles said. "But I am finding it difficult to reconcile the German proclamation of defence against the 'imperial aspirations of the British aggressor', whilst gunboats are threatening our French allies."

Kurt Heiss leaned back in his chair and crossed his legs.

"Perhaps I may begin by assuring you that our beloved Kaiser Wilhelm has the utmost respect and admiration for the British people." Kurt Heiss said. He paused for a moment then said mildly. "The colonial expansion of France and Britain has gone uncontested for decades. Do you feel that, in light of this imperial expansionism, that Germany is at fault for not accepting this premise?"

"But that is silly." Simon Charles said. "The German merchant navy have repeatedly abused their position in the world to flood our colonies with cheaper goods at the expense of our home markets. Even more alarming was the unprovoked attack of SMS Panther in Morocco."

"Gunboat diplomacy." Lord Vellance murmured.

"My dear sir, the newspaper reports of this incident were greatly exaggerated." Kurt Heiss said. He sighed with great patience. "It was indeed a gunship, certainly nothing as large as the Dreadnought ships produced by Britain and with which Britain has dominated the high seas."

The lights in the smoking lounge flickered for a moment. I could see the unease of the steward as the airship shuddered.

"The wind seems to be picking up." I said to no one in particular.

"You are entirely correct Mr Heiss, regarding the dominance of our Dreadnoughts." Mr Potts said. "It is a proud tradition of seamanship that our beloved country has. It is what has made Britain great."

"Your gunship was a threat against our trade routes in that area." Simon Charles said.

"Come now." Kurt Heiss smiled. "We were merely enforcing our claims in the area. Your own state department had previously advised France that its own actions were unwise. Negotiations are ongoing. A logical agreement will result once compensation for Germany is agreed."

I could see why Kurt Heiss had been chosen as a diplomat for Germany. He was relaxed in the face of several angry Englishmen. As a Welshman, I was amused by their reactions.

"Are you going to Agadir?" I asked.

"No. I will be departing the airship in Paris and returning to Berlin from there. I received a telegraph recalling me for some urgent discussions, which is why I have chosen to travel by airship for the first part of this journey."

"What urgent discussions?"

I hadn't seen Herts appear. He took a seat next to Simon Charles.

"If I knew what the discussions were about, I doubt that they would be quite so urgent." Heiss smiled politely. He raised his glass and signalled to the steward for another drink.

I doubted that I would need my wits over the next few days so I offered to buy one for him. He smiled a thank you and joined me in a glass of Jameson whiskey.

The conversation had moved on to cricket. That particular obsession was not one that I shared so I pleaded ignorance and retired to a comfortable sofa and read the London Standard. I was glad to see that I no longer appeared on the front pages of this illustrious gazette.

The RMS Olympic had launched on her maiden voyage to New York. Captained by Edward Smith, it would take a week to sail the Atlantic. I shook my head at wonder at the largest ship in the world. Although slow compared to an airship, it was a floating hotel.

"May I have a moment of your time?"

I looked up from my newspaper in surprise but the question was directed towards Mr Herts. Lord Vellance sat next to him. In my defence, I did try to ignore their conversation, I did try to read the newspaper, but my curiosity was too strong.

Lord Vellance was silent for a few moments. He had taken off his gold framed spectacles to polish them and looked very young and innocent without the spectacles framing his face.

"Penelope has retired to our room, so I thought this might be an opportune moment for us to discuss some things. Clear the air, so to speak."

Herts nodded but said nothing. He folded his newspaper.

"See hear, Reginald." Vellance continued. "You need to remember that she is your sister. I had hoped that when I married into your family that I would..."

"That you would what?" Reginald Herts asked. "Continue to leech off me? Continue to beg money from me? I have supported you and my dear sister long enough."

Lord Vellance sprang to his feet. His face was flushed, his hands clenched.

"You must not speak to me in that tone." Vellance said.

His voice was low and angry. He turned and strode to the bar. He gulped down a large whiskey and then left the smoking lounge.

Herts watched, an ugly sneer twisted his face.

I hurriedly returned to my newspaper, appalled at his shocking attitude.

I left the smoking lounge a few minutes later. It was late in the evening and I was feeling tired. Kurt Heiss had started to play whist on the gaming table. He returned my goodnight with a goodbye. The airship would be arriving in Paris six o'clock in the morning and I would not see him until he returned to London. We cordially exchanged cards and I returned to the sitting room.

As I entered the sitting room the door to the promenade deck burst open. I helped one of the crewmen shut it before turning to the ladies with a rueful grin. The rain had swept in and soaked me.

Elisabeth was kind to fetch a towel from a steward.

"Thank you."

I sat between Elisabeth and Dorothy Heiss. Unlike her husband, Dorothy Heiss did not have a German accent. I sat listening to her discuss knitting and crochet with Mrs Colchester. Apparently there is a difference between knitting and crochet. Who knew.

"Mrs Fabersham has not returned." Elisabeth said.

"It is late." I said. I knew what she really meant was that Roland had not returned from escorting Mrs Fabersham to the bedroom wing. "I see that your Aunt Imogen has already retired, perhaps we all should retire. We will have several hours in Paris tomorrow."

Elisabeth agreed and, after bidding the ladies a good night (and Dorothy Heiss a goodbye), I escorted her to her bedroom. My bedroom was in darkness. I had forgotten to wind the clockwork light earlier when I changed for dinner.

I wound the clockwork light then changed into my nightshirt in its pale glow. I sat for a moment, the wire bed squeaking in protest, then stood. The room did not have a clockwork extractor fan, so I opened the porthole gingerly before lighting my cigar. I watched the storm rage outside.

Lightning flashed across the sky. Thunder rolled in pursuit.

When I was young I had been afraid of thunder and lightning. I had been taught from the pulpit that the sheer ferocity of the storm was God expressing his anger at the sins of the world.

The belief in God's justice no longer comforted me.

I fell asleep quickly in the surprisingly comfortable wire bed. The storm rocked me to sleep. I did not dream thankfully. My dreams of late had been dark, full of promises of death. The night terrors had haunted me recently.

I slept until the screams woke me.

Chapter Five

I was on my feet reaching for my clothes before the second scream sounded. I dressed quickly, slipping my feet into my bedroom slippers. From the corridor outside of my room I heard a hubbub of voices. "I will get the doctor" was shouted outside my door, and I heard heavy footsteps departing.

I was frantic. I could hear Elisabeth stepping into the corridor to investigate. I abandoned my cravat, leaving it forlorn on the bed and wrenched open the door.

A third scream echoed along the corridor.

I ran towards the stern of the airship, to the last door in the bedroom wing. A crowd had gathered at the entrance. I pushed through the crowd, using a commanding voice.

A maid had fainted in the corner. Lady Vellance attended her.

The room was actually a suite of rooms. The entrance opened into the sitting room. Silk sheets covered the drab canvas walls. Brightly coloured dancers flitted across the walls as the silk swayed in a breeze. There was a small round porthole on the far wall. It stood open and I could see that the storm still raged outside. There was a travelling trunk flung open in one corner. A valise next to it, lay empty on its side where it appeared that the storm had tossed it. A bottle of opened red wine stood forlorn on a small table. There were no glasses, I noted.

I looked finally at the dead body in the centre of the room. It belonged to Reginald Herts.

"Step back. Give me room." I said to the onlookers.

A man was attending the body. I could smell a familiar sweet smell emanating from him. He was a member of the crew.

"I am Doctor Peters." The man said, peering up at me.

I introduced myself.

Reginald Herts had a peaceful expression on his face. He was fully dressed. The only sign of blood was a thin, red mark in the centre of his chest.

"Stabbed through his heart." Doctor Peters said. "It would have been quick. I doubt he felt a thing."

"He is still wearing shoes." I said. "It must have happened shortly after he returned to his room."

"What is going on here?"

The voice belonged to the captain as he pushed his way into the room past the crowd. He paled when he saw the dead body. I stood and caught him by the arm, steadying him.

"Clear the room." I called. "This is now a crime scene."

I extracted my identification card from my wallet and showed it to the onlookers. It took a few moments to clear the room, by which time the captain sat in the chair. The doctor was standing uncertainly beside him.

"Do you need me for anything?" Doctor Peters asked. "I need to check on the maid."

"Of course doctor, thank you for helping." The captain shook his hand.

The doctor left the room. Through the opened door I caught a glimpse of red hair. Elisabeth was arguing with one of the stewards. I excused myself and strode across to the door to speak to her.

"Elisabeth. This is not an appropriate place for a young lady."

"I already saw the dead body before you asked us to leave." Elisabeth said. "I've not fainted like that fool of a maid, nor am I scared of blood. I can be of assistance to you."

"Your Aunt Imogen would not approve." I said.

"I have already asked her." Elisabeth said. "I told her I could help you. The murderer is here among us, you will need all the help you can get. I can be useful. I can make notes and drawings."

"It is really not appropriate." I said.

"Why not?" Elisabeth asked. "I can write better than most men I have met and I'm meticulous."

I stopped and thought about it for a moment. I did need the help. If this was in the centre of London, I would have a junior detective making notes of everything that was said, every move I made. She was a little pale but, as she said, she had not fainted.

"You did promise to be my chaperone. This way you can look after me."

"You had better get some paper and a pen." I said. I was awarded by a flash of dimples.

A few moments later, Elisabeth returned armed with a pen and some pink writing paper. I directed her to sit at the table, moving the bottle of wine to the side. She had a man's fountain pen. I raised my eyebrows at this.

"My father left it to me in his will." Elisabeth explained. She composed herself at the small table.

I glanced at my pocket watch. Then nodded to Elisabeth to start writing.

"The body was discovered at eight o'clock in the morning by the maid. Her screaming alerted the passengers and crew to the murder of Reginald Herts. I found a crowd in his bedroom gathered around the dead body. Doctor Peters, the airship physician, was attending the body and confirmed that he was dead."

I spoke slowly, watching Elisabeth writing each word as I dictated it. Her script was fast but fair and she nodded to me to continue when I paused.

"The room is a large cabin, with canvas walls covered by silk. There is a second room adjoining." I paused for a moment and stepped over to the door into the next room. It was a bedroom as I suspected. "That room is a bedroom, no one has used the bed. There are no other exits from this suite that I can ascertain. I am checking the canvas walls to ensure that they are whole."

It took me a few moments to check all the walls. There was no tears in the canvas, no secret entrances, no hidden way to enter the suite.

"The bedroom has a large window which is securely latched. The sitting room has a porthole." I crossed to the porthole. The floor was damp with rain next to it. I could see a pile of ash. "The porthole appears to have been open all night. There are traces of cigar ash so I assume that the victim was smoking."

There was a clockwork smoke extractor fan on the wall. I wound it slightly. I could hear the clockwork motor turning, but could not feel air being extracted.

"The extractor fan is broken. There is a trunk belonging to the victim in the corner. Unopened." I opened it. There were some clothes and a small shaving kit. I closed the trunk. "There is also a small brown valise. It is open and empty. There is a bottle of wine on a small table. It has been opened but there are no glasses."

Elisabeth looked up.

"Is that a clue?"

"It might be." I said. "But then again, he may have drunk the wine straight from the bottle. At the moment I am merely recording my observations. My old sergeant used to tell me 'make a note of everything, you never know what is a clue'."

I knelt by the body and lifted the arm. It was stiff to the touch.

"The body is lying in a state of repose. It is slightly stiff so I would suggest that Mr Herts has been dead for several hours."

"Since late last night?" Elisabeth asked.

"I can't say that for certain." I said. "Although the storm has cleared the air, it is still quite warm, so it would be difficult to say exactly what time."

The airship shuddered slightly as if to remind us that the storm still raged outside.

"The body is fully dressed including his shoes." I paused for a moment. "That's odd."

"What's odd?"

"His waistcoat. The buttons have been done up wrong."

"Perhaps he dressed for bed, then changed his mind?"

"Then he would not have laced his shoes up again, unless he intended to walk the promenade deck." I shook my head. "It was very stormy outside, it would not have been a pleasant walk. Make a note of it now. It is certainly a clue."

I checked the pockets of Herts's jacket. His pocket book was present and had the princely sum of thirty pounds in one pound notes. A small box of cigars was in another pocket with a lighter. His pocket watch was in his waistcoat, the second hand ticking merrily, unaware that its owner was dead. A white handkerchief concluded his pockets. I listed these items for Elisabeth.

I rolled the body over to check for any other wounds. There were none however, from his right hand a dark brown, clay pipe slipped free. I studied it thoughtfully. It had an intricately carved detail on the stem. I sniffed it. It had not been lit for some time.

"Perhaps he had smoked a pipe as well." Elisabeth said when I mentioned it.

"No." I said. "It is another clue. If Mr Herts had smoked a pipe, we would have found pipe-cleaners in his pocket and a pocket knife. I have never seen a pipe smoker without a pocket knife. They need it to dig the burnt tobacco from the pipe, you see."

I wrapped the pipe in my handkerchief and placed it in my pocket for safe keeping.

"There are no other stab wounds." I said. I stood up. My back ached from rolling the dead body over. "Mr Herts has a single stab wound through the heart. There is very little blood. There are no weapons in the room so the murderer either took the weapon with him, or threw it out the porthole."

Elisabeth looked up from her notes.

"But there was a weapon." She said. "When I entered earlier there was a pair of silver scissors sprouting from his chest."

I looked wildly around the room. There were no scissors. The murderer had taken the weapon from under all our noses.

Chapter Six

During my career as a detective, I had always found that the first few hours after the murder were crucial to finding the killer. In this case however, there was nowhere for the murderer to escape to. My old sergeant used to say, follow the clues and interrogate the suspects, the murderer always made a mistake.

Always.

I had several clues to start with but as yet no idea what they meant, and the murder weapon was missing.

I strode to the door, wrenching it open.

The steward was at his usual station. He was the same steward I had bid a polite goodnight to several hours earlier. I beckoned for him to approach.

"Is there a place where we can store the body?"

"Yes sir. There is plenty of room in the balloon section of the airship. I will need to confirm with the Captain though first."

"Fetch some men to move the body, if the Captain approves." I said. I paused for a moment in thought. "We were supposed to arrive in Paris early this morning. I assume that we are late because of the storm, can you confirm with the Captain when we are due to arrive?"

"Yes sir."

I watched the steward hurry away.

"Is that relevant?" Elisabeth had approached me silently from behind.

"We were supposed to arrive in Paris at six o'clock in the morning." I replied. "The murderer may have timed it so that they could leave the airship in Paris before the body was discovered. The storm however has delayed our arrival."

"Therefore, if we can confirm which passengers are due to leave the airship at Paris, we can confirm who the killer is." Elisabeth said.

"Possibly." I said. "If the murderer is intelligent enough, it might be the opposite. The murderer may decide that staying on-board is the less risky step to take. We cannot make this assumption without some evidence. It is highly indicative, however."

I could see along the corridor that the steward was returning with two burly stewards. They were carrying a stretcher between them.

"Ahh, he returns. Gather your writing paper and pen, we are going to have some breakfast with your Aunt Imogen and leave these fine gentlemen to guard the suite."

I stepped aside to allow Elisabeth to precede me from the suite. The three stewards waited politely, one of them touched his forelock as Elisabeth strode past.

"Keep this door locked until I return." I said to the steward. He nodded, his young face impassive.

I stopped at my room and changed into my suit jacket and added my cravat. Psychologically I would be at a disadvantage if I appeared under dressed.

Breakfast was a quiet affair. My cousin Imogen had wakened to the shocking news of the murder, somehow she had slept through the screams and hubbub. Kurt Heiss was speaking quietly in German to his wife Dorothy when I entered. He smiled when he saw me and invited us to join him.

"I can but assume that you are investigating this horrible affair." Kurt said. "Do you have any clues yet?"

"Just the one or two." I said. "Forgive me but I will need to keep things close to my chest while I investigate."

"Quite right."

"I do have the able assistance of my cousin, Elisabeth." I said, I gestured to Elisabeth beside me. "I think she will be invaluable in helping me follow the clues and question the suspects."

"Do you think it's appropriate for a young lady to be helping you investigate this horrid crime?" Imogen said.

I turned and gave Elisabeth a hard stare. She looked down and tackled her fruit bowl silently.

"I do need someone to help me." I said. "Someone I can trust."

Elisabeth blushed. I was angry at her for lying about having her Aunt's permission. I did however need her assistance.

"You mentioned suspects." Kurt said. "Can you tell me who are your suspects?"

"You are." I said. I gave him a direct look then shrugged. "In fact everyone on this airship is a suspect, including Elisabeth. Elisabeth is the least likely to be the murderer. Not because of her age or gender but because she has never been exposed to the criminal element."

"Does that mean that Aunt Imogen is a suspect as well?" Elisabeth asked, her voice subdued.

"Everyone is." I confirmed.

The discussion changed to other matters. Kurt Heiss kept us entertained with stories about his travels. At the other tables I could hear that the discussion about the murder was on-going. People were naturally speculating as to the identity of the murderer. Naturally

Kurt Heiss, as the representative of the German government, was at the head of the very short list.

Captain Harvey approached our table at the end of breakfast. I invited him to sit.

"The suite belonging to Reginald Herts is now empty. One of the stewards is guarding the door."

"Thank you." I said. "When will we arrive in Paris?"

"The storm winds became too fierce and drove us back during the night." The captain said. "We have returned to Dover to wait for the winds to abate. Because of the murder, I now intend to return to London when the wind dies."

I thought for a moment. The airship was an international vessel therefore the jurisdiction on-board would be whatever the captain decided. It was comforting however that we had returned to England.

"Would you mind that I continue investigating?"

"Thank you, yes. If there is anything that you need from me?"

"Can you give me a list of the passengers." I said. "Also I would need to speak to the maid, the steward, and the doctor if that could be arranged."

The captain readily agreed.

"Also, would I be able to send a radiotelegraphy message back to London?"

I spent a few moments composing the message on a pink slip of paper borrowed from Elisabeth. The captain accepted this. He made an announcement to the rest of the passengers regarding the delay in the voyage. A sigh went around the room. He returned to the bridge.

We were trapped on board the airship with a killer. In my experience a killer, once trapped or threatened, would kill again. We did not have much time to find him.

Chapter Seven

After breakfast, I wished my companions a good morning and led Elisabeth to the suite. Doctor Peters, the steward and the maid were waiting for us. The body had already been removed.

At my request, the steward disappeared for a minute or two, then returned with several chairs. We sat in a circle. Elisabeth had returned to her table and was waiting expectantly, her pen poised over the pink sheets of paper.

"Doctor, if I can start with you." I said. "How long have you practised medicine?"

I gently drew his history from him. He had studied medicine in London but had found it difficult to establish a practice there. He had jumped at the chance to become a ship's doctor when the post became available. It was an easy job which paid well.

"Normally I dispense airsickness tablets, or treat a cough." He concluded.

"Did you meet or talk to Mr Herts prior to finding his body this morning?" I asked.

"In fact I did." Doctor Peters replied. "He approached me late last night and asked for a tonic. He said his stomach was unsettled from the storm and he needed something to help him sleep. I gave him a gentle sedative."

"What time was that?" I asked.

"It was after the game of whist had finished." His face screwed up slightly in thought. "He was one of the players. That would have been about ten o'clock in the evening."

"He went straight to bed after that?"

"I recommended that he go straight to bed. I myself went shortly after. The storm was making it uncomfortable to walk and there was a general consensus from everyone to retire to bed."

"Who was playing whist, do you remember?" I asked.

"Mr Reginald Herts, Mr Simon Charles, Mr Kurt Heiss, and Lord Horace Vellance."

"Ahh, sir." The steward coughed then interrupted us. "I did see those four gentlemen come down the corridor together. I don't rightly know what time it was. They seemed a bit drunk."

"Thank you." I said. I motioned him to be silent and he subsided.

"The sedative, would it put him to sleep immediately?" I asked the doctor.

"No sir, it was a mild sedative."

"He had been drinking alcohol, whiskey if I recall correctly, could the sedative had knocked him for six?"

"No sir. I deliberately gave him a very light tonic for that reason."

"Did he drink the tonic in front of you?"

"Yes sir, and had another whiskey as a chaser."

"Who called you this morning?" I asked.

"The steward did." Doctor Peters indicated the steward sitting beside him. "I heard the screams from my office and came to investigate. He met me on the way. Mr Herts was already dead when I arrived."

"The cause of death?"

"He was stabbed through the heart." Doctor Peters said. "I checked his pulse just to make sure, but he was already dead."

"What was he stabbed with?"

"It was a pair of scissors. They were silver. I removed them myself from his heart."

"Where are those scissors now?" I asked.

"I do not know. I left them next to the body."

"They were missing when I arrived, where are they?"

I pounded on the table. Doctor Peters jumped slightly.

"I do not know. I left them there. I was too busy attending the body."

"Think, man. It is very important."

Doctor Peters shook his head.

I wanted to shake him. I resisted the sudden impulse. The doctor was smaller than me by a head. In fact, he was smaller than Elisabeth. He sported a brown goatee on his face which had been tugged gently into a point. Perhaps he wore it in an attempt to hide his youthful looks. There was a slight mark on the upper part of his nose.

"Where are your spectacles?" I asked.

He patted his right pocket automatically.

"They are still in the office." Doctor Peters replied. "I have not returned to the office since this morning."

"Were you wearing them yesterday evening when you were reading?"

"No, sir. I only wear them when my eyes are tired."

I nodded and dismissed him. He breathed a sigh of relief and left the suite. I eyed the steward and the maid. They both quailed under my gaze.

The steward was a large man with an open face and gentle blue eyes. His uniform must have been tailored to fit him, he had such a large frame it could not have been easy finding clothes to fit. He sat poised on the edge of his seat with his large feet firmly planted under him. His body language was interesting as well. Rather than face me direct, he was half turned in the chair, protectively I thought, towards the young maid.

The maid was very young for her position. She had a round face, her eyes red with recent tears. Her hands were clasped on her lap and she squirmed nervously under my gaze. She was also sitting at the edge of the chair but her feet were turned slightly towards the door, as if she was ready to flee.

"How did you know he wore spectacles?" Elisabeth asked, interrupting my train of thought.

"The marks on his nose." I said. "He had forgotten to wear them last night. If he needs them for reading, it is possible that he gave Mr Herts the wrong sedative."

I turned to the maid.

"Young lady, what is your name?"

The maid confirmed her name was Elisa Pitt, she had worked for the company for two years, this was her second voyage on the Airship Arcadia. She sounded as timid as she looked. My voice softened as I asked her questions.

"You knocked on the door at eight o'clock sharp, is that correct?"

"Yes sir. Mr 'erts had requested for some 'ot water for shaving this morning. 'e was very strict about the time."

"So you knocked on the door and then opened it when there was no answer?"

"Yes, sir. Just like that, sir."

"Tell me what happened next."

The maid paled slightly. She glanced towards the steward who nodded reassuringly.

"I opened the door with my right 'and. My left was holding the jug of water. I just opened it and then, and then -"

She broke off, and looked at me in mute appeal.

"Go on." I said.

"It was 'orrible, sir." The maid said, her words came out in a rush. "'e was lying there, all still like. I could see the scissors all sparkly in 'is chest. It was just 'orrible."

"That is when you screamed?"

"I screamed and I came all faint. Rodders 'ere came rushing up. Then all the other passengers came rushing in to see what was 'appening. I must 'ave fainted then. I woke up in my room with Doctor Peters giving me some smelling salts. They were 'orrible too, they woke me right up."

I glanced at Elisabeth, waiting for her to catch up. She glanced up from the pink pages and nodded to me.

"Did you see anyone pick up the silver scissors?" I asked.

"I didn't see no one, sir."

The maid looked ready to cry so I allowed her to return to her duties. It is a weakness of mine. I could never handle a woman crying. I always feel that I should be doing something to help other than the empty words 'there, there'.

The steward moved his feet uncomfortably.

"Your name is Rodders?" I asked.

"Rodney, sir." The steward's voice was quite high pitched, which was unexpected for a man of such a large frame. "Rodney Jones, but everyone calls me Rodders."

He had a very open and honest face, and a very expressive one. He had been with the company for just over a year. He had worked his way up from stoker in the engine room to his current position as steward. Passengers found his presence a comfort, he had been informed, especially late in the evening when they were drunk and needed assistance to their rooms.

"That was your job, to help people to bed?" I leaned back in my chair crossing my legs.

"Not just that, sir. I am the night steward. If a passenger requires something during the night I am there to help him as best I can."

"You were there all night?"

"Yes sir. I don't stir from my chair."

"You said you saw Mr Herts return to his room drunk after his game of whist. Did anyone accompany him to his room?"

"Not that I saw, sir." Rodders said. "It was a busy time for me. I was helping people to their bed, and not always to their own bed, if you know what I mean, sir."

I coughed and glanced meaningfully at Elisabeth who had stopped writing and was looking wide-eyed at the steward. The steward blushed and muttered an apology.

"And you did not see anything unusual?"

"Not then, sir. No."

"Not then?"

"It was about two hours later, sir." Rodders said. "I was just returning to the bedroom wing when someone walked past me towards the promenade deck. He was all dressed up with a heavy coat, hood pulled across his face. I thought that's queer, going out in weather like that."

"I thought you said you did not stir from your chair?"

"It was only for two minutes." The steward's voice became defensive. "Mr Charles asked me to fetch a tonic from the doctor for airsickness. I was bringing it back and met Mrs Potts. She was looking for a pot of tea."

"Did you recognise the man?"

"I didn't see his face, sir. Do you think it was the killer?"

"Why didn't you ask him who he was?"

"We're all supposed to be discreet like."

I thought for a moment. The worst possible luck. If the steward had questioned the mysterious figure, or at least recognised him, the case would have been solved.

"Did Mrs Potts see the masked man?" I asked

"He almost bowled her over. I was helping her to her room."

"Then you gave the tonic to Mr Charles?"

"Yes, sir. Mr Charles was at the door waiting for me when I turned around."

"Was there anything else unusual during the night?" I asked.

The steward though for a moment and shook his head slowly.

"Nothing else last night." Rodders said. "I heard a crashing sound from Mr Bakerson's room this morning. A chest of drawers had toppled over from the storm. I knocked on the door and, when he answered, I could see clothes strewn across the floor."

"But nothing else? Even the smallest detail might be important."

Rodders shook his head.

"Tell me about this morning."

"Elisa delivered the hot water at eight o'clock, as she said. She was worried about being late. I heard Mr Herts speak sharply to her last night asking for her to be on time. I was talking to Mr Ashton at the time when I heard her drop her jug and scream. We both raced to Mr Herts's suite and he was there, dead as can be. I ran to bring the doctor and the captain."

"You left Mr Ashton in the room alone?"

"He was patting Elisa on the wrist. She had fainted. Other passengers were coming out to see what all the fuss was about."

"You met the doctor. He was on his way?"

Rodders nodded. "He opens his surgery at eight o'clock every morning. He had heard the screams and was running to see what was happening, as was everyone I guess."

"Very well," I said. I thanked the steward and ushered him towards the door.

I turned my chair around to face Elisabeth. She waited, an expectant look on her face.

"What happens next?" Elisabeth asked.

"First, we talk." I said. I bit my lip, I hated what I was going to say. The words stumbled out. "This morning. At that door. You lied to me."

Elisabeth shook her head, not a denial of the lie, but in embarrassment.

"You lied about having permission from your Aunt Imogen to help me with the investigation." I said. "I am very grateful for your assistance but I need to feel that I can trust you. Can I trust you?"

She nodded. I raised an eyebrow.

"Yes, you can." Elisabeth said.

I lie to myself all the time. I tell myself I am all right, that I can do this, that I can get through each day. It is all lies. It was ironic that I should be explaining to her about the importance of truth.

A knock on the door interrupted my thoughts and a steward announced Mrs Colchester. I invited her to sit. For once she did not have her knitting with her. She sat primly on the edge of the chair facing me, her silver hair neatly coiled in a bun.

"I have a confession to make."

Chapter Eight

I blinked.

As a young constable in the constabulary, my sergeant regaled us with stories about criminals who were so remorseful of their crimes, they approached the desk sergeant in the police station and told him that they had a confession. This had never happened to me. That is, before today.

"You have a confession?" I asked stupidly.

Behind me I could hear the scratch of the pen stop. Elisabeth waited expectantly.

"I know I should not have done it but, in an irrational moment, I panicked." Mrs Colchester said. "I have never done anything like this but I did not want to get into trouble so, when my panic subsided, I returned to confess."

Mrs Colchester sat with an air of expectancy. I glanced at Elisabeth who shrugged.

"Forgive me, Mrs Colchester." I said carefully. "What exactly are you confessing to?"

"The scissors, of course." Mrs Colchester said. "It was my scissors which killed Reginald Herts. I recognised them when the good doctor pulled them from the dead body and placed them to the side."

Mrs Colchester paused for a moment and withdrew a handkerchief from her pocket. The handle of a pair of scissors peeked from the handkerchief.

"I panicked when I saw the scissors. I knew that they were my sewing scissors. When the doctor placed them next to the body, I panicked. I had to steal the scissors back before anyone else recognised them and I was blamed for the murder."

I took the scissors from Mrs Colchester's hand. I could feel her hand tremble. I opened the handkerchief and glanced at the bloody point, then turned and placed them on the table next to Elisabeth.

"When did you lose your scissors?"

"I do not remember, sometime yesterday."

"Perhaps we can start at the beginning." I said.

My voice was gentle as I questioned her about her past. She was extremely wealthy. Her husband had owned a string of shops which passed to her when he died. Her son had died in the Boer war so she had no one to inherit her fortune. Instead she was following her doctor's advice to seek warmer climes for her health.

She knew of Reginald Herts. Her husband had business dealing with him before he died.

"What did Reginald Herts do?" I asked. This was one of the questions I had radio-telegraphed to London. We had yet to receive a reply.

"He did anything to make money." Mrs Colchester said. Her lips twisted. "He supplied my husband's shops with pharmaceutical supplies which we sold to doctor surgeries. My husband, God rest him, mentioned that he had been involved in trading weapons with various governments. If there was a war, he could be found selling weapons to both sides."

"You do not seem sorry that he is dead."

"No, I am not." Mrs Colchester said. She glanced across at Elisabeth. "You look shocked, my dear. He lived by the sword and he died by the sword. I often thought that the rifle my son carried, when he fought in the Boer war, was probably supplied by Reginald Herts. But so was the bullet that killed him."

I looked at Mrs Colchester for a moment, not speaking. The laughter lines on her face had disappeared, to be replaved with wrinkles and a careworn expression. A face, that had seen such joy and laughter now, showed only grief. I resisted the urge to lean forward and pat her hand. She had the means to kill Mr Herts, the scissors, and she now confessed to having a very strong motive for killing him.

"Did you murder Mr Herts?" I asked simply.

I heard the scratching of the fountain pen stop.

"I could have, you know." Mrs Colchester said. "When you get to my age you are no longer afraid what people think of you and what life can do to you. Life had already thrown the worst at me with the death of my little boy."

"Did you murder Mr Reginald Herts?" I asked, a little more softly.

"No, I did not."

The scratching resumed.

"Tell me about last night. I escorted Elisabeth to her room at about nine o'clock in the evening. You remained in the sitting room discussing crochet with Dorothy Heiss?"

"Yes. I find it very difficult to sleep so I usually stay awake until rather late. I spoke to Dorothy who is such a lovely girl. We exchanged crochet patterns." Mrs Colchester paused in thought for a moment before continuing. "Roland Ashton joined us later in the evening for a drink before retiring to his bed."

"Roland returned?"

I could hear the hope in Elisabeth's voice. Mrs Colchester heard it too.

"Roland is a queer duck, Elisabeth. He talked about travelling to different countries, including New Zealand. I have visited New

Zealand. He was lying about his experiences. You do not want to trust such a man."

"What time did Roland go to bed?" I asked.

"I am not sure. The game of whist had not finished, so it was before ten o'clock."

"Do you recall who else remained in the sitting room?"

"Mrs Potts was there but she did not speak much. Her husband was reading the newspaper. He retired before me. Lady Vellance was there until late, waiting for her husband. She sat next to the window reading a book by the electric light. You do know she is royalty, I suppose. Her husband is fifteenth in line for the throne of Lichtenstein. I knew his father, such a lovely man. I suppose you have heard of the term 'land rich but cash poor'? That describes Lord and Lady Vellance."

"Who else was there?" I asked.

"The lovely Edith Charles sat in one corner talking to Mr Bakerson. I do not know why, for he is such a brute."

"I thought that he had been confined to his cabin?"

"I thought so too." Mrs Colchester said. "But -"

A knock interrupted her and the captain entered.

"Sorry to disturb you but I have received a radio-telegraphy message from London." He handed it to me. "As you can see, I have been ordered to proceed at best speed to London once the storm abates. It has been requested that you continue your investigations until we arrive."

"When will we arrive in London?" I asked.

"It is unlikely that we will be able to cast off until tomorrow."

The captain nodded politely to the two ladies and left.

"Interesting." Mrs Colchester said. I raised an eyebrow. "I wonder why the Captain bothered to walk all the way here with the telegram instead of asking a steward to deliver it."

"He feels impotent." I said. I rubbed my chin thoughtfully. "He is a man of action. He feels frustrated by the lack of action. A man has been murdered on his airship but he has nothing to do."

"Where were we?"

"Mrs Colchester was about to tell us about Marcus Bakerson." Elisabeth said.

"Ahh yes, Mr Bakerson." Mrs Colchester said. She frowned. "He appeared in the sitting room shortly after Roland Ashton joined us. He approached Roland, apologised to him and shook him by the hand. Mr Bakerson then sat by the window and Mrs Charles joined him shortly thereafter."

"When did you go to bed?"

"It was after the game of whist had finished, I am not sure what time that was. Mrs Potts was still up. When you get to our age, you do not need much sleep."

"Just a few more questions." I said. I felt around in my pocket. "Do you recognise this?"

I handed Mrs Colchester the pipe that I had retrieved from Mr Herts's hand.

Mrs Colchester unwrapped my handkerchief and examined the pipe. She shook her head slowly before handing it back.

"It is quite an unusual colour." Mrs Colchester said. "Most pipes are black, this pipe is a burnished brown. I bet whoever lost it would be quite eager to find it again."

I bet he would be. I would love to see his face when I hand it to him. I rewrapped the pipe and replaced it in my pocket.

"Last question." I paused for effect. "Who do you think killed Mr Herts?"

"You will probably think I am a little bit silly." Mrs Colchester said. "I overheard the argument shortly after dinner. They were arguing about money. Mr Herts made several cutting remarks, and then he threatened to kill Reginald Herts."

"Who did?" I asked.

"Lord Horace Vellance." Mrs Colchester said. "It was Lord Vellance who killed Mr Herts."

Chapter Nine

"This is utterly preposterous." Lord Vellance said.

After the interview with Mrs Colchester, Elisabeth and I knocked on Lord and Lady Vellance's suite. We were admitted to the sitting room by a maid while Lord Vellance changed his jacket. Elisabeth took the opportunity to sit at the table with her writing paper.

The steward was called and had arranged three chairs for us in the sitting room by the time Lord Vellance emerged. He was still wearing the same suit although the wrinkles in the suit had disappeared. He dismissed the maid and sat opposite me.

"Unfortunately my wife Penelope has taken a turn and will not be joining us." Lord Vellance said. "This frightful business has upset her and the doctor has offered her a tonic and recommended rest."

I murmured my apologies.

I questioned him closely about the reasons for his trip. His older brother had passed away unexpectedly last year and he had been thrust into the management of the estate. He was travelling to Rome to visit a small vineyard he had inherited.

"I was informed that you had an argument with Mr Herts yesterday evening after dinner." I said.

"An argument? Good Lord, no. It was a discussion, merely a discussion."

"Merely a discussion in which you told Mr Herts that you would kill him?" I asked.

Lord Vellance removed his gold framed spectacles and started to polish them with a handkerchief. His movements, I noticed, were very jerky.

"Now look here, what exactly are you accusing me of?"

"Murder. Did you kill Mr Herts?"

"This is utterly preposterous." Lord Vellance said. He replaced the glasses on his face. "Do you know who I am? I am a peer of the realm. You cannot accuse me of murder."

"Did you kill Mr Reginald Herts?"

"This is silly. I demand that you apologise to me at once. It is an outrage that you can simply waltz in here and accuse me of murder. I simply will not stand for it."

He leapt to his feet and dramatically pointed at the door. I rose slowly to my feet. Elisabeth stood uncertainly.

"It is a simple question and one that you have refused to answer." I said. "Did you kill Reginald Herts?"

"It is beneath me to answer it." Lord Vellance said. He stormed over to the door and held it open. "I am a gentleman and will refuse to answer such a question. Please leave."

"Certainly, sir." I smiled at him pleasantly. My chest grew tight as my bottled rage threatened to overcome me. "Come along, Elisabeth. You are my witness. He has refused three times to deny he is the murderer. The papers will find that of interest I feel."

Lord Vellance paled at the thought of the scandal.

"You would not dare."

I ushered Elisabeth in front of me, allowing her to leave first.

"Wait." The strangled cry had come from behind me. I turned. Lady Vellance had entered the sitting room from her bedroom. Her petite face was drawn and rather pale. "Please wait."

I waited. At a nod from Lord Vellance, I returned to my chair and Elisabeth to her table. I remained standing until Lady Vellance, with assistance from her husband, sat in the chair opposite.

"This is a murder investigation." I said. I rudely cut Lady Vellance off as she was about to speak. "I need you to answer every question I ask. Answer truthfully. Do not think of me as Ignatius Brown, that entertaining chap who regaled you with the police adventures. I am here in the guise as Detective Sergeant Brown of the Scotland Yard constabulary. I am the Law."

I paused and waited for Lord Vellance to nod. Lady Vellance was clasping him by the arm. I suspect that I was one of the few men to have spoken to Lord Vellance like that in his life. I could see that I had made an impression on him so I relented.

"Let us begin again." I said in a soft tone of voice. "Did you kill Mr Reginald Herts?"

"No."

"Nor I." Lady Vellance said.

"But you did threaten to kill him?"

"Yes I did, but it was not like that." He paused. I could see he was thinking, debating exactly what he could tell me.

"Tell me truthfully."

"It was a new venture. I was trying to get him interested in investing in our vineyard. It is quite small but in a beautiful place overlooking Rome. It is a fantastic opportunity. It just needs an influx of new capital. Someone to invest in the venture."

"In fact." I paused for a moment then turned to face Lady Vellance directly. "In fact, Reginald Herts was your brother."

"How did you …?" Lady Vellance stared at me in shock. I was not going to mention to her that I had overheard part of a conversation the previous evening.

"You thought your brother would invest?"

"Reginald is, or rather was, my brother." Lady Vellance said. She waved distractedly towards her husband. "We heard that he was travelling to Rome on business by airship and decided to join him. We thought it would give us a chance to talk to him properly. Make the proposal. At the very least he could view the property before making the decision."

"But he rejected you."

"He rejected Horace, but I was going to appeal to him again in the morning." Lady Vellance linked her arm through her husband's and drew him close. "We were never close, Reginald and I, but we were still family."

"There are other people you could borrow money from. Why not appeal to them?"

Lord Vellance laughed harshly.

"Do you think we have not tried?" He asked. "The difference between the gentry and the lower classes is that the gentry have a better class of creditors."

"So you are in need of money and approached Mr Herts to invest in your venture." I leaned back in my chair. "Tell me about your brother, Lady Vellance. Is he married? Does he have any children?"

"No, and no." Lady Vellance said. "He has a suite in Pall Mall close to his place of business in the centre of London and has girls living there. But he is unmarried."

"So, who would inherit his money now that he has been so tragically murdered?"

Lady Vellance gaped at me in shock. The thought of inheriting from Herts had not occurred to her. I could tell by the expression on her face she only now realised that she had a motive for murder. Either she was a brilliant actress or the shock was genuine. It took her several seconds to find her voice again.

"I would. I mean, it sounds a lot worse than it is."

I raised my hand to cut her off.

"You can see why it is so important for me to conduct these interviews."

Lord Vellance nodded dumbly. Lady Vellance's hands were white where she gripped his arm.

"Perhaps I can ask about last night." I said. "Lord Vellance, you played whist with Mr Herts until late?"

"Yes. We finished the last game at ten o'clock then decided to retire for the night."

"How are you so certain that it was ten o'clock?"

"Kurt Heiss, he is that amiable chap from Germany, was leaving the airship at Paris and did not want to stay up too late. He had arranged with the steward to remind him at ten o'clock."

"Then you went straight to bed?"

"Yes. No, not straight away." Lord Vellance paused in thought. "Simon Charles insisted on buying us each a whiskey as a thank you for a memorable evening. We drank it, finished our cigars and proceeded to bed."

"Did Mr Herts play all evening?"

"He did. He was partnered with Simon Charles for most of the evening and seemed to have quite the stroke of luck. I am glad that he sat next to the smoke extractor, he never stopped smoking those damnable cigars. He drank the whiskey and left with us."

"Did he not visit the doctor before he left for bed?"

Lord Vellance raised his eyebrows in surprise. He looked like a young boy who had been caught out in a lie.

"Why, I suppose he did. The doctor was reading in the corner and Herts walked over and demanded a tonic for an upset stomach. The doctor returned as quick as you like and Herts threw it back followed by his whiskey. We then went to our separate bedrooms, Herts still belching out his cigar smoke like a steam train."

"That was the last you saw of him?"

"Yes it was."

"Lady Vellance, I believe you were reading for most of the night. Can I ask what were you reading?"

"It is a newly published volume." Lady Vellance said. She rose and stepped over to a small bag in the corner returning with a familiar book which she handed to me. "The Biography of Dr John H. Watson. It is rather an entertaining read. I find his writing quaintly amusing."

I smiled as I accepted the book. I glanced in the flyleaf and noted the signature.

"I have the same book. It is difficult finding the time to read it however." I said. "He wrote an inscription and signed it for you as well?"

"John is a dear friend." Lady Vellance said. "My father was a patient of his for several years."

"I am glad that you are enjoying the book. How long did you read it yesterday evening?"

"The electric lights in the sitting room are so much brighter than the clockwork lights in this suite. I sat reading in the sitting room until the men finished playing their last game of whist. I preceded them to the bedroom wing."

"Did either of you leave your suite during the night?"

Both Lord and Lady Vellance shook their heads murmuring no.

"You did not see any mysterious figure in the bedroom wing late in the evening?"

"No."

"Your bedroom is quite close to Mr Herts's suite. Did either of you hear anything suspicious during the night?"

"I did hear a crash this morning but I did not think anything of it." Lady Vellance said. "I thought that it was perhaps just the storm had caused something to tip over."

"But nothing else?"

At the shake of their heads. I produced the clay pipe and passed it over, still wrapped in the handkerchief.

"Do you recognise this?"

Lord Vellance removed his gold framed spectacles in order to examining the pipe closely. His face, suddenly innocent without the spectacles, screwed up in thought.

"I have seen similar pipes but not one exactly the same." Lord Vellance said. "Is it a clue?"

He handed the pipe to his wife who returned it to me. I noted that Lady Vellance had barely looked at the pipe. Was this significant? Was there a reason that she did not need to examine the pipe?

"The pipe was found in Mr Herts's room. I am merely following up to see if it is relevant or not." I said. "Did Mr Herts smoke a pipe?"

"I have only seen him smoke cigars." Lord Vellance said.

"Perhaps." Lady Vellance said. "I do not know. I cannot remember. When we were young we had an uncle who liked to smoke a pipe, so perhaps Reginald decided to try."

"Perhaps he did." I said. "One last question."

I paused. Their faces brightened in the hope that this interrogation was ending.

"Who do you think killed Mr Herts?"

"It could have been anyone." Lady Vellance said. "He was not a very likeable person."

"I think it was Kurt Heiss." Lord Vellance said. "You cannot trust these foreign chaps. Don't get me wrong, Kurt is a very nice man, for a German that is, but he is just not as civilised as us English. I mean he does not even play cricket."

I refrained from telling Lord Vellance that I did not play cricket either.

"I think Kurt Heiss is a spy. He is so friendly, but then he asks a question and you find yourself telling him everything about yourself."

"Reginald sold weapons." Lady Vellance said. "Perhaps Mr Heiss was buying them for Germany and they had a falling out."

"So you think Mr Heiss is the killer?"

"Mrs Colchester too." Lady Vellance said. "Did you know that her son died in the Boer war? I know for a fact that Reginald sold those weapons to the Boers in South Africa."

"I would look at Marcus Bakerson." Lord Vellance said. "Did you see how he put his head together with Herts? There is something going on there, I would say."

I nodded towards Elisabeth. We both got up.

"Sorry about the unpleasantness earlier but, you understand my duties." I spread my hands wide in an apology.

"Not at all." Lord Vellance murmured.

I allowed Elisabeth to precede me from the cabin.

"What do we do next?" Elisabeth said, once we were alone.

"Now we interview Mr Heiss." I said in a confident tone.

I did not feel confident. It seemed that everyone had a reason to kill Reginald Herts.

Chapter Ten

I found Kurt Heiss and his wife Dorothy in the sitting room discussing the weather with my cousin Imogen. Through the sitting room windows I saw heavy rain lashing the promenade deck. Several figures, wearing heavy rubber waterproofs, struggled with lines.

I expressed my apologies to Imogen at neglecting her and invited Kurt and Dorothy to a private table in the dining room. Through an open door to the kitchen I could hear the faint clatter of kitchen utensils as the cooks prepared our lunch.

A servant girl brought us some tea and fresh scones.

I began by asking them about their background. Kurt was kind enough to speak slowly to ensure that Elisabeth could keep up with writing.

Kurt Heiss had been born in Bremen, Germany. His father was a business man who travelled frequently to London. That explained why his English was almost flawless. He now lived in London working as a diplomat to the English crown.

"Although tensions between Germany and England are high, you are still our biggest trading partner." Kurt Heiss said. "It is to our advantage to ensure that the lines of communication remain open and frank."

"I heard it said that war was merely another form of diplomacy, and that peace was the resting time between wars." I said, goading him.

Kurt Heiss smiled and leaned back, a small cigarette in his hand.

"That is why diplomacy is so delicate sometimes. As a diplomat, I am striving to obtain the best solution for my country. My counterpart in London is trying to do his best for England. Where we have an imbalance between our two desires, the possibility of war always exists."

"I have heard the accusation that you are a spy for your country not a diplomat." I said. "That would surely be a motive for the murder of Mr Herts."

Kurt Heiss laughed.

"I have often heard the same accusation that all diplomats are spies. You are the first to actually say it to my face."

"Are you a spy for Germany?"

"What is a spy?" Kurt Heiss held up his hand to forestall a reply from me. "A spy is someone who obtains information for his country usually in a clandestine way. My job, my raison d'etre, is to obtain information that is helpful to my government in a timely basis. I do not obtain that information in a clandestine manner, not least because I do not have time. My daily schedule is too busy. Does that make me a spy?"

"Did you know Mr Herts?"

"I knew of him. Part of my assignment is to contact local businessmen and open new discussions about trade with Germany. Although I have never dealt directly with Mr Herts, I heard about the types of goods and services that he offers. Not the sort of services for which we would be willing to pay."

"You mean weapons?"

"Not the weapons themselves." Kurt Heiss said. He continued in a delicate tone. "His price for the weapons included the delivery of the weapons to countries that required them."

"You mean he was a gun smuggler?"

"I was trying to say it a little more diplomatically than that. We did not require his services as a gun smuggler."

"And you, Mrs Heiss?"

"Mr Herts was not in the same social circle as us." Dorothy Heiss said. "Although I never got the opportunity to meet him, I heard of the type of person he was. Quite a horrid individual."

"Did either of you kill Mr Herts?"

I could see by Kurt Heiss's expression that he found the question distasteful.

"I do not make it a habit of killing people." Kurt Heiss said. "Although, as a diplomat, I could have shot him and there would be no repercussion. Remember, I have diplomatic immunity."

Dorothy Heiss placed her hand over her husband's.

"Neither of us killed Mr Herts." Dorothy Heiss said. "Kurt is too accustomed to speaking with other diplomats to answer a question directly. I can see from your expression that you are not accustomed to such indirect talk."

I nodded thanks to Dorothy Heiss. My chest had begun to tighten with anger. She was right. I hated indirect answers.

"Can I take you back to yesterday evening." I said in a pleasant tone. "You were playing whist until late?"

"That is correct. As Dorothy and I were intending to transfer in Paris to the Berlin train, I wanted an early night. I asked the steward to remind me at ten o'clock which he duly did. We drank a last whiskey, then retired."

"Who won?"

"I am not sure. Mr Herts was certainly delighted with his winnings although it was Mr Charles who bought us a celebratory whiskey at the end of the night."

"You drank the whiskey and then went straight to bed?"

"Yes. No. Actually Mr Herts had complained about an upset stomach, perhaps a touch of airsickness. He left his drink on the table and approached the doctor for a tonic. The doctor had been sitting nearby taking advantage of the electric lights. He got up at once and arranged it for him. We then retired for the night."

"You were talking to Mrs Colchester for most of the evening Mrs Heiss?"

"She was quite delightful company actually." Dorothy Heiss said. "She was teaching me a new crochet pattern. She kindly allowed me to use some wool and practice the stitch."

"Did you use her scissors?"

"We did not finish the garment that we were working on so there was no need. Why?"

"Her silver scissors have been identified as the murder weapon and you had access to the scissors."

"Yes, I did." Dorothy Heiss said. "As did many other people who visited us. The knitting basket was to the side of Mrs Colchester's chair and was unguarded."

"Did many people visit your table?"

"During the evening, nearly everyone I think." Dorothy Heiss said. "Especially at the end of the evening when people came in to bid us a good night."

"Did you see anything odd or suspicious last night, or hear anything during the night?"

They both replied to the negative.

"I did not see you this morning. Did you hear the screams?"

"We both wakened early as we were expecting to leave the airship in Paris." Kurt Heiss said. "As the arrival had been delayed, we took the opportunity to enjoy an early breakfast in the dining room. We heard the screams and saw the doctor rush from his surgery to the bedroom wing. We arrived at Mr Herts's door in time to see everyone in the process of leaving it."

He shrugged. "In this day and age of suspicion and pointing fingers, suspicion would lie naturally on my door. I did not want to be involved."

I stirred my tea thoughtfully for a moment. They had the means to steal the murder weapon, and a possible motive. As a gun smuggler, Herts would have access to some of the countries that Germany had expanded into. Germany naturally would be unhappy with someone who armed the rebels.

I shook my head. This was silly. I was building a wild theory out of nothing. If Germany had wanted Herts dead, it would have been much easier to knife him in a dark alley rather than stabbing him in a suite with a pair of scissors.

"Who do you think killed him?" I asked.

Kurt Heiss leaned forward to stub out his cigarette, then leaned back again.

"I have no idea. Anyone that I accuse would naturally point back to me and say 'He is German, he did it.' I refuse to play that game."

I reached into my pocket for my handkerchief.

"One last question." I said. I pulled out the brown pipe and unwrapped the handkerchief. "Do you recognise this?"

Kurt Heiss gave a startled exclamation in German and leaned forward sharply.

"That is mine."

Chapter Eleven

Kurt Heiss reached for the brown pipe. Instinctively I pulled it away.

"The pipe is evidence." I said. "I found it in Mr Herts's suite. Can you tell me how it got there?"

"I reported the pipe missing yesterday evening." Kurt Heiss said. "The steward said he would inform the captain and make sure that they kept an eye out for it. What was it doing in Mr Herts's suite?"

"I was hoping you could tell me." I said. "I found it clutched in Mr Herts's hand. Are you sure you lost it earlier in the evening? Why would Mr Herts be clutching the pipe when he was murdered?"

"I lost it before the game of whist. You can check with the steward." Kurt Heiss said. He leaned back and calmly regarded me over his tea cup. "It is an obvious attempt to cast the blame on me when you think about it."

"Possibly, or perhaps this was his only way of telling us who was about to kill him." I said.

That explanation sounded hollow even to me. If Herts had known he was about to be stabbed, all he had to do was raise his voice and the large steward would have come barrelling through the door.

Kurt Heiss regarded me as I reached for my own tea cup. The tea had gone cold but it was in my nature to drink tea when I can, regardless of the temperature. I sipped, the cool liquid tasted bitter.

"Do you have any more questions?" Dorothy Heiss's voice was as cool as the tea I was drinking.

I shook my head and stood.

"You have been very courteous in answering my questions." I said. I motioned for Elisabeth to join me. "I regret the nature of my questions and I will take no more of your time."

I left Kurt and Dorothy Heiss in the dining room drinking tea. I had more questions now than I had before I started. The most obvious was who would want to frame Kurt Heiss and was he really innocent?

*

I found Simon Charles and his wife Edith in the sitting room. They were sitting at a separate table playing cards at a small table. I apologised for disturbing them and joined them. A separate table was provided so Elisabeth could continue to take notes without disturbing their card game.

"You had quite a run of luck with the cards last night." I said.

Simon Charles smiled.

"Whist is not a game about luck, it is about experience. It is about judgement, understanding your fellow players. I played a game of whist at my club every Thursday night for almost twenty years. That is twenty years of understanding the psychology of my opponent. I would hazard a guess that even a Detective Sergeant such as yourself would not have the same level of experience against your opponents."

I heartily agreed. Understanding my opponents was very important in my line of work.

I started the interview by asking the usual question of who they were and why they were on this trip. As they answered, I found myself stealing glances at Edith Charles. That same dazzling smile that transformed her face was playing on her lips. Simon Charles informed me that he was a lawyer travelling to Paris to finalise the purchase of a property for a client.

Edith Charles smiled again.

"I insisted on joining Simon on this trip. I mean, it is gay Paris, the fashion centre of Europe. I just had to come on this trip to renew my wardrobe for the autumn season."

She certainly looked very fashionable sitting next to her drab husband. He still dressed like a funeral director.

"Do you get the opportunity to go on many business trips?" I asked.

"This is the second such trip this year." Simon Charles said. "The last one was to Rome. It was winter there. Beastly cold. I was glad to return home."

"Have you met Mr Herts before yesterday?"

"I did see him once before, at a social function." Simon Charles paused in thought. "It was last December, I believe. My office always has a Christmas party where we entertain our clients and any potential clients whose business we wanted to solicit. He was present at the party, but I do not know if he was an existing client of the partners or a new client. I did not speak to him then, nor have I seen him since."

"And yourself, Mrs Charles?"

"I would hardly have the opportunity to meet him and, he is someone that you would remember." Mrs Charles said.

There was something about her accent that did not sound quite right but I could not put my finger on it. It sounded almost practised. I nodded politely and tucked that thought away for now.

"Can I ask you to cast your minds back to the events of yesterday evening." I said. "You were playing whist, Mr Charles, for most of the evening. Tell me about it."

"I was partnered with Mr Herts for part of the evening, sitting directly opposite him in fact. I spent most of the evening studying his expression to get a hint of how he was playing."

"I thought it was only the psychology of the opponent that you were interested in?" I asked.

"The comment of keeping your enemies close and your friends even closer becomes even more relevant in the game of whist." Simon Charles said with a laugh.

Perhaps it was just me but, with Simon Charles dressed almost like a funeral director, his laugh seemed ghoulish, out of place. I nodded for him to continue.

"Mr Herts played a very close hand. He dropped a couple of cards that he should not have and was lucky that Lord Vellance did not pick up on his mistakes."

"The game finished at ten o'clock. What happened then?"

"It did seem to finish early. I was willing to play on, but I could not entice that doctor fellow to join the game."

"You bought a celebratory round of drinks, I was informed."

"We bought each other drinks." Simon Charles said. He beamed. "I did win a few pounds. Lord Vellance was not doing very well. I think Mr Herts had bullied him into playing, and he did play quite poorly. But he is rich, he can afford the losses."

"Then what happened?"

"My wife joined me and I took myself to bed."

"Did you notice anything unusual during the night, strange noises, people walking around?" I asked.

"Nothing at all I'm afraid."

Mrs Charles shook her head as well. She flashed dimples again.

"The steward mentioned that you were feeling unwell later?"

"Oh yes, that would have been sometime after midnight." Simon Charles said. "The storm was buffeting the airship quite badly and I was feeling a little airsick. I asked for a tonic. He was gone for so long, I had to chase after him."

"Did you see anyone else in the corridor?"

"No one. Oh wait, I did see Mrs Potts very briefly. The steward was helping her to her room."

"The steward mentioned that a mysterious figure had brushed past him. Did you see anyone bundled up in the corridor?"

"Not last night."

"Did anyone leave their rooms last night while you were in the corridor?"

"I was only in the corridor for a few moments when I made the request of the steward and again when I chased him up."

I gritted my teeth in frustration. The murderer had managed to kill Mr Herts and escape. The only other person who had seen the murderer was Mrs Potts and I was not convinced that she was a reliable witness.

"And you, Mrs Charles. You spent part of the night talking to Mr Bakerson?"

"I had met him once before and was renewing my acquaintance." Mrs Charles said. "He does have a brutish appearance but beneath that he is quite shy."

Shy? That was new to me. Marcus Bakerson had a bad reputation for violence and blackmail. I wondered what social circles they shared. I could not imagine that Bakerson was part of her sewing group.

"Did you talk all evening? What were you talking about?"

"Mutual acquaintances. I grew up in a street near him. We talked only for a short time before he retired for the evening."

"You were both awake early this morning to depart the airship for Paris?"

"Yes, we both had breakfast instead of leaving. That is, until the screaming started."

Dorothy Charles froze. She had a look of surprise on her face.

"It is funny. I am only thinking of it now. Kurt Heiss and his wife were at breakfast as well. When the screaming started my husband and I naturally bolted immediately to the door. I remember looking back at Kurt Heiss. He had not moved. He was sitting at the table and continued to butter his toast. He had a peculiar expression on his face. It wasn't surprise. It did rightly give me the chills."

Chapter Twelve

"You forgot to ask them who they thought had killed Mr Herts." Elisabeth said.

We had begged the steward for a pot of tea and rejoined my cousin Imogen at a table in the sitting room. I accepted another buttered scone. The wind died down and I could hear the other passengers discussing the murder.

Everyone, that is, except Kurt and Dorothy Heiss.

When they had entered the sitting room and sat at a table. I noticed people moved away. I do not know if it was subconscious or not, but the other passengers had decided to shun the German couple. A growing circle of empty chairs appeared with them at the centre.

"No I did not. It was obvious they would blame the Germans." I said. I turned to Imogen. "Would you mind if we moved seats?"

"Surely you don't mean to move away from them, Ignatius?" Elisabeth asked. "That is totally unfair. They are such a charming couple."

"Not away." I assured her. "I would like to join them. They deserve a presumption of innocence."

I lifted our tray and we moved across to join the German couple. Kurt Heiss received us with a raised eyebrow.

"You were regaling me yesterday evening about your adventures in East Africa with your dachshund." I said in a loud voice. "I mentioned this to my cousin Elisabeth and promised her you would tell us more."

Kurt Heiss gave me a grateful smile. As he began again to tell us about his African safari, I noticed that the conversations around us had resumed to their normal levels. Only the occasional dark look at us. I excused myself after ten or so minutes and asked the steward to direct me to the captain.

I found the captain in the wheelhouse at the helm of the airship. There were large windows both to the front and side of the wheelhouse. A large map occupied the back wall. There was also a window in the floor with a railing to stop anyone from accidentally stepping through.

That sweet smell, that all the ships crew wore, permeated the wheelhouse. It was almost suffocating, and I had the urge to hold my nose in a most undignified manner.

The captain was talking through a blower with someone in the engine room. He patted a large steering wheel next to him absent-mindedly. He signalled to me to wait for a moment.

"We may need the engines sometime during the night." Captain Harvey said.

There was an affirmative on the blower and the captain replaced the instrument on its hook. He turned to face me.

"Sorry about that. What can I do for you?"

"Will we be returning to London this evening?" I asked.

"I am hopeful." Captain Harvey said. He gestured towards a stool and I made myself comfortable. "I received a radiotelegraphy message from the London office. They informed me that the storm was slowly starting to clear over London, and they expected us to begin to travel again late this evening."

"That is a relief." I said. "Have you received any radiotelegraphy messages for me?"

"Not as yet."

Captain Harvey stood and walked to a small table near the entrance. There was a pot of tea on a tray with some scones and sweetmeats. I declined the tea but accepted a buttered scone. My figure will hate me.

"I did want to ask if you could perhaps allow me a small favour." I said. "The porthole to Mr Herts's cabin was open when I entered it this morning. I want to examine the outside of the porthole to confirm if this was used as a method for entrance or exit."

"Can you not examine it from the inside?"

"I need to examine it from the outside as well." I said. "The wind has died down so now might be an opportune moment to do this while everyone is enjoying their tea."

The captain heaved himself to his feet and walked to the window on the port side. I could see that it was still raining outside though not as heavily as before. He returned to the blow tube next to the wheel and used it to summon one of the men from the engine room. We waited until he appeared.

"Yes sir?"

The man that appeared was quite young and slim but very well muscled.

"Mr Johnson. I want you to rig a cradle for Mr Brown here, and lower it over the stern of the airship. Mr Brown is the detective, he wants to examine the outside of the airship."

"I can do that for you sir." Johnson said.

I said my thanks to the captain and followed Johnson up a flight of stairs. After a short climb, we entered the balloon itself. It was very hot. The hot air from the steam engine was funnelled into the airship to provide the helium sacs with extra lift. My nose was assailed by the most awful smell.

"What the devil is that smell?" I said.

"That's the smell of oxen entrails." Johnson replied, with a laugh at my discomfort. "Don't worry your 'ead sir, you do get used to the smell."

I followed him across a metal gantry. The gantry stretched in the distance, criss-crossed at different places. There were hundreds of tall thin sacs in-between each gantry, each containing helium. Above me I could see the ribs of the balloon, the skin pressing tightly against it.

Johnson led me towards the rear of the balloon. I noticed that we passed several hatches in the floor. At my enquiry Johnson confirmed that those hatches would give external access to different parts of the roof of the passenger car of the airship.

"Just for inspection in case there are any problems." Johnson said.

He collected a long line of rope with a stirrup seat and attached it to a winch. He gave me a wind-breaker to wear to protect my clothes from the rain. I stepped into the stirrup and belted it tight.

"You'll be as safe as 'ouses sir." Johnson said. "We do this all the time. Every time we return to London we inspect the old girl just to make sure she is still airworthy. We don't normally do it in weather as rough as this but you should be fine."

With these reassuring words, he threw open the hatch. I do not normally suffer from a fear of heights, but I do have a healthy respect for them. I looked down at a height of about fifty feet to some fir trees that were stretching their branches up to reach me. They swayed violently in the wind. The noise was horrendous. The hatch was positioned at the very end of the passenger car so I would be lowered to pass within touching distance of its stern.

"That's just the sound of the wind through the trees." Johnson said. "Nothing to worry about there."

With one end of the rope attached to the winch and the other attached to me, I was slowly lowered through the hatch. The wind immediately caught me and sent me spinning. The world passed in a blur for several very long seconds until I felt the edge of the passenger car with my feet.

I grabbed at the passenger car and used it to steady myself as I was lowered. My head was dizzy. The porthole was to my left and I shouted to Johnson. The wind swept my voice away but Johnson must have understood my gesticulations. With a shudder of the rope, I was dragged to the left. I signalled to Johnson to stop.

The porthole looked smaller from the outside that it did from the inside. I examined it inch by inch. Searching the smooth metal for scratches, for any indication or reason that it had been forced open. The smooth metal offered no clues. At my signal Johnson released the rope to swing freely and I swung to the big window of Mr Herts's bedroom. Again there were no scratches.

I signalled to Johnson to pull me up and he bent to the task of turning the winch. I walked my legs along the side of the passenger car to guide me.

Suddenly the wind caught me. I was flung me back. I heard a shout from above. I slammed into the passenger car. Hard. My left leg was on fire. My breath rushed out. The wind caught me again. This time I started to spin. I could not breath. The world passed me in a spinning blur.

I retched.

Then Johnson grabbed me by the shoulder and the spinning stopped.

"Are you all right, sir? You seemed to have taken a bit of a knock."

Johnson continued to wind the winch and, once I was level with him, he kicked the hatch closed, and unhitched me from the stirrup seat.

"You look very pale, sir. Let's get you out of that wind-breaker and a good soothing cup of tea into you."

Johnson led me back to the wheelhouse. He sprayed me with something sweet smelling.

"To get rid of the smell from upstairs." He said.

I had banged my bad leg on the passenger car and it felt like it was on fire. I limped slightly.

"The wind caught 'im good sir, but 'e should be alright in a jiffy."

I sat in the seat offered to me by the captain, and accepted a cup of tea. My hands were still shaking and the spoon rattled in the saucer. The captain pretended not to notice.

The belief that everything would be alright with a cup of tea cannot be understated. The familiar taste. The warmth. The calm liquid that soothes you like no other drink can.

I did not refuse the splash of rum the captain added to it.

"Did you find anything?"

"Nothing." I swore softly. "Nothing at all."

Chapter Thirteen

The tea service had been cleared away by the time I returned to the sitting room. I apologised to my cousin Imogen for my absence. She replied with an exasperated 'hrumph'.

The wind picked up again and I raised my voice to join the conversation.

"Who are we going to interview next?" Elisabeth asked.

I glanced around the room. Mr and Mrs Charles enjoyed their tea at a nearby table. Mr and Mrs Potts occupied some soft seats near the window where they watched the storm.

"Mr and Mrs Potts." I said loudly over the noise of the storm. "Mrs Potts was in the corridor with the mysterious stranger. She may have seen something significant."

Elisabeth excused herself for a moment and returned to her room. She reappeared a few moments later with her pink paper and fountain pen clutched in her hand. The fountain pen must have been recently recharged as I could see that it was dripping ink.

I excused myself from my cousin Imogen and the Heiss couple and crossed the sitting room to Mr and Mrs Potts.

"Do you mind if I pose one or two questions to you?" I asked.

"Only if it is one or two questions, young squire." Mr Potts said.

His face however creased into a large smile as he waved me to a soft chair. Elisabeth perched next to a handy table.

Although quite elderly with grey hair, Mr Potts proved to have a lively mind. He had kept himself acquainted with the news in the London Standard and was quite pleased to have a famous detective interviewing him.

Mr Potts owned a shipping office in Plymouth. He worked with managers from all around the world, buying and selling goods, and transporting them back to England. He was travelling to Paris and Rome to meet some of the managers with whom he had only corresponded by telegraph. He was worried about the anti-German sentiment, as it would impact trade.

"Have you ever met Mr Herts in your line of work?" I asked. "He buys and sells weapons and transports them to different countries. Has he ever tried to arrange a cargo with your shipping office?"

"I know of him, but I have never met nor worked with him." Mr Potts said. He drew himself up proudly. "Our family has a strong tradition of never transporting or buying and selling weapons. He and his kind are leeches on society."

"You have strong views on this."

"Very strong views. Modern society seems to have a moral disconnect when it comes to selling weapons. They sell it to the wrong tribe and are surprised when that tribe now massacres another."

"How do you feel about the murder of Mr Herts?"

"I am saddened that he is dead. The bible teaches us that killing, for any reason, is wrong. But I must confess that there is a certain satisfaction that he died the way he lived, with violence."

I saw Elisabeth shift uncomfortably in her chair.

"If I can ask you to recall last night." I said loudly, the rain was battering heavily against the window. "Can you give me a brief account of your actions last night and anything relevant that you may have seen?"

"There is not much to tell. I had dinner with my wife Victoria, then listened to the entertaining discourse about the 'Case of the Missing

Cat'. You are very good at giving lectures. After that-" Mr Potts paused for a few moments in thought. "Ahh yes, I stayed in the smoking room. There was that frightful attack on Mr Heiss. Just because he is German it does not mean that every German complaint should be laid at his door. After that I joined my wife then went to bed and slept until morning."

"And you Mrs Potts, can you tell me about your evening?" I said loudly.

Mr Potts repeated my question loudly into her ear.

"It was a ghastly evening." Mrs Potts said. "The soup was cold and I am quite sure that waiter gave me the wrong dessert."

I explained to her that I meant after dinner.

"I am getting to that." Mrs Potts said. "Youngsters these days do not have any patience."

"You were saying?" I suppressed a grin.

"After dinner I sat in the sitting room listening to Mrs Colchester and Mrs Heiss talk about crochet. They had the pattern all wrong I fear. My husband joined me later and read the newspaper to me. I was not tired so I stayed up watching the storm. I must have fallen asleep, the steward woke me and fetched me some tea. Then I went to bed."

"Did you see anyone with Mrs Colchester's scissors?"

"Her scissors? Someone said they found her scissors in Mr Herts's room. A terrible thing. I expect he stole them."

"Did you see anyone near her basket?" I asked.

"Basket, who's basket?"

I refrained from rolling my eyes. I am quite proud of that. I know I am frequently short with people, I am not a people person, but I do make an effort to be nice to the elderly. Not least because I hope to survive long enough to be elderly one day. I tried to smile as naturally as possible.

"Mrs Colchester's knitting basket?"

"What about it?" Mrs Potts asked.

"Did you see who took the scissors from Mrs Colchester's basket?"

I was nearly shouting by now what with the sound of the storm outside and Mrs Potts's deafness. Imogen gave me a disapproving look from across the room.

"No," Mrs Potts replied, "should I?"

I shook my head rather than answering.

"When you went to bed, did you see the mysterious figure who bumped into you?"

"Oh yes, I thought he was a member of the crew. It was such terrible weather last night I am not surprised he was so bundled up."

"Yes it was." I shouted. "Did you see who it was?"

"No. I told you, he was all bundled up." Mrs Potts replied. "I was very surprised at the footwear though."

At that moment, there was a tremendous crash. A shudder went through the frame of the airship and I felt the buffeting increase as the airship slid sideways. A young crewman dashed through the doorway.

"The airship has broken free of her anchors." He shouted, his face alight in panic. "We need everyone to help re-secure her."

This is when I made my next mistake. I forgot to ask Mrs Potts what she meant.

Chapter Fourteen

The next hour was a nightmare.

The front anchor had not been properly secured and the storm had ripped it from the ground. The airship spun in a dizzying circle before it caught again. However the airship was now side-on to the wind, the deck started to heel over under the relentless pressure of the gusts.

I tumbled to the ground, the chair snapping under me. I threw myself to the side and managed to catch Mrs Potts. We slid together across the sitting room, towards the other side. Elisabeth supported Imogen at the door. She stared in horror as furniture rushed towards her. I heard a distant yelp of fear from Mrs Charles as she tumbled together with her husband, a tangled mass of arms and legs.

The airship snapped upright as the wind abated.

I pushed myself to my feet and helped Mrs Potts to the door. I exchanged a glance with Mr Charles. We nodded to each other, the crew needed help.

I wrenched open a door, telling Elisabeth tersely to stay here and help the ladies and Mr Potts to hold on. I led the way into the corridor.

The corridor was in chaos. There were several stewards shouting conflicting orders: shouting for help; asking people to brace themselves; trying to lead volunteers to protect the airship. I waded forward and pushed through the frightened crowd.

Roland Ashton and Kurt Heiss were already there, volunteering to help. The steward led us out to the promenade deck which was awash with rain. There were four lines arrayed across the deck as several crewmembers tried to deploy four new anchors to the ground.

As I watched, the ship heeled over again, caught in another strong gust of wind. The line on the port side had four sailors on it. As I watched, they staggered to the side then tumbled to the ground, losing their footing. I ducked as the line whipped free across the deck.

"Grab the line." Someone shouted.

I grabbed it then swore aloud as the rope slid free, burning the palm of my hand. Then Kurt Heiss was beside me, then Roland Ashton, then Simon Charles. We managed to stop the line slipping and braced ourselves.

The four sailors had picked themselves up and ran across the deck to join us. I recognised Johnson and he flashed me a grin. We pulled at the line. Eight of us throwing our weight and our muscles into holding the airship as the rain soaked us and the wind buffeted us. Finally it was secure.

I wrapped a handkerchief around my palm before joining the next line. The airship shuddered. The wind continued to pick up. That's when it happened.

The line snapped.

Eight of us were holding the line and, as one, we tumbled to the ground having lost the tug of war with the wind. I rolled towards a hatch door and grabbed hold of it just as the airship heeled over again.

I looked across the promenade deck. Instead of the horizon, I found I was looking at the forest below. The airship continued to heel more and more on its side and everything, including people, started to slide towards the edge.

I hesitated.

I know that future accounts will tell of how I threw myself across the deck, slid to a halt next to another hatch door, and saved the life of a sailor, pulling him to safety. The truth is I hesitated.

Obviously the fear of dying had crossed my mind. More striking still was the fear of failure. The fear that I would miss and that he would die regardless of what I did. Or perhaps I would not cross the sloping deck athletically enough and dislodge the sailor from his precarious perch and knock him to his death.

I hesitated. He almost died because of it.

The deck slowly righted itself. The sailor shook my hand and got up. I lay on my back staring up at the balloon above the promenade deck. It acted like a sail, catching every gust of wind. We needed somehow to turn the airship.

I sat up. A second line had been secured on the starboard side. Johnson helped to tie it off. I went over to him and shouted in his ear.

"We need to turn the airship around."

"What?"

"The airship. We need to turn it so its nose is facing into the wind."

"It's impossible. We have lost those anchors. The wind is too strong."

"Then we need to turn it so that the stern is facing the wind." I shouted. "The airship won't survive side-on into the storm."

Johnson grabbed me by the shoulder and together we staggered towards the lines on the port side.

"We can double down on the lines we have holding the stern." Johnson shouted. He lifted a fire axe from its hooks on the rail.

"When I give you the signal I want you to cut this line. We will let the wind work for us and turn us around."

I stood by the rail watching the crew attach a new line. A member of the crew was lowered on a cradle. He started spinning on the cradle before he left the deck. They had lost the anchor so he was to tie the line to a tree or a strong outcrop of rock.

The rain was coming down in steady sheets and I lost sight of Johnson and the crew on that side of the airship. It seemed an eternity of waiting before I got the signal to release the line. Kurt Heiss joined me at the rail. He held me steady when the airship heeled again in the relentless wind.

We were both thoroughly soaked by the time the signal came. The fire axe struck true and the line whip-lashed out to the darkness.

I stumbled to the deck. I felt a sharp stab of pain on my left leg as I landed heavily. Kurt Heiss thankfully caught the fire axe and we clung together as the airship spun for a moment before settling. We had saved the airship.

"Well done." Roland Ashton said as he helped us to our feet.

I replaced the fire axe on its hooks and returned to the sitting room with Kurt Heiss, through the sitting room doors, to a hero's welcome.

I brushed my feet mechanically on the rug, my shoes making wet impressions on the floor. Towels were provided to us and we dried ourselves off as best we could. Simon Charles was already there, getting the attentions from his wife.

I got a hug from Elisabeth who, I noticed, gave Roland a quick hug as well.

"You should be very careful taking such a risk." Imogen said. "You could have been hurt."

I didn't mind. Imogen only scolded when she was worried. I showed her the palm of my hand. The friction from the rope scored a burn across the palm. It was dark red and already starting to blister.

Cousin Imogen pretended not to notice how much my hand was shaking. She spread some salve on it, cream to calm the skin. Her soothing words calmed me. When you try and calm a frightened dog, it's not the words that calm it but the tone of voice used. It was the same for me.

I had almost lost it. The fear of failure had almost caught up with me. What if the next time I freeze? What if I do not act and, by inaction, cause someone's death.

Again.

Imogen's soothing words were almost as good as a bandage over my soul. It took several minutes (and a large glass of Jameson's whiskey) and I was ready to face the world.

But I had yet to face the killer.

Chapter Fifteen

Imogen insisted that I drink a cup of tea.

It was not as if she was part of the Temperance Movement, with their prohibition on the consumption of alcohol. She was in favour of drinking in moderation ... but still allowing people to drink. But she always said that, in her experience, a strong cup of tea instead, would clear the cobwebs away.

I caved in.

The stewards quickly stood the tables and chairs upright. Imogen, Elisabeth and I took the first set nearest the window so I could look out across the promenade deck.

"Do you have writing paper and pen?" I asked Elisabeth after a few minutes of comfortable silence.

Elisabeth returned after a few minutes and placed them on the table.

"Do you mind if I take a few moments to interview you, Imogen?" I asked.

Imogen sat primly on her chair.

"Of course dear, what would you like to know?"

"Did you know Mr Herts before you came onboard the airship?" I asked.

"I have seen him a couple of times briefly before in London. It was at the … oh, let me see." Imogen paused for a few moments, her brow furrowed in thought. "The first time was at a ball. It was given in honour of Lord Vellance's father. I do not know why Mr Herts was there, but he was pointed out to me."

"He is, or was, the brother of Lady Vellance, and theefore Lord Vellance's brother-in-law. That's why he would have been invited I imagine. Why was he pointed out?"

"It was gossip." Imogen said. "You should know that gossip travels faster than a steam engine."

"I know that gossip travels around so fast that they could use it as an alternative power source instead of steam." I said.

Imogen gave me the look she reserved for children. I raised my hands in mock self-defence. Elisabeth giggled.

"What did the gossip say?" I asked.

"It said, and this is only gossip mind, that he was a weapons smuggler, and that he was smuggling weapons into German East Africa. Our government was turning a blind eye to his activities as it destabilised the German rule and promoted British values in the area."

"So the German government would have a reason to kill him." I said.

I thought back to how Kurt Heiss had supported me on the promenade deck, and his firm handshake when we both returned to the sitting room.

"Not just him of course." Imogen said. "There were two others at the ball who were also weapon smugglers as well. They would have been interested in getting rid of the competition."

I was impressed and said so. Imogen would have made a good spy, her contacts seemed to know everything.

"You mentioned that you had seen him twice?" I asked.

"Yes, quite recently in fact. I took a notion last week to purchase some new dresses for Elisabeth. I happened to visit a cafe in the centre of London to meet an old friend. Herts was sitting in the cafe as if waiting for someone. I recognised him at once, of course."

"Did your friend not have some juicy gossip about Mr Herts?"

"Oh no, he doesn't gossip."

I was instantly intrigued. My cousin Imogen doesn't usually visit London for shopping and certainly not to visit old friends. Who was this gentleman friend? Unfortunately it did not have any relevance to the murder so I did not have an excuse to satisfy my curiosity.

"So you didn't really know Mr Herts?"

"He was a horrid man. I am glad that I never made his acquaintance. I am sorry that he has died but I think the world is a better place without his presence."

"So you didn't know Mr Herts, certainly not enough to have any motive?" I asked.

The scratching at the table stopped.

"Are you asking Aunt Imogen if she killed Mr Herts?" Elisabeth asked in a shocked tone of voice.

"I am asking her if she had a motive for killing Mr Herts." I said. "Do you?"

The question was to Imogen. For a moment I imagined she was about to say something but then she shook her head.

"Of course not. I barely knew the man."

"Moving on to last night." The scratching at the table had resumed. "Did you see anyone at Mrs Colchester's sewing basket?"

"No, I did not."

I winced. Imogen's voice had grown cold.

"Did you see anyone acting suspicious?"

"Mr Bakerson seemed to have a relationship with Mr Herts. He also seemed to be a bit of a thug, have you asked him?"

"Not yet." I said. I pointed to a list of names I had received from the steward. "I am going through the passengers in a methodical manner, depending on their distance from Mr Herts's cabin. You retired to bed early, before I returned from my lecture. Did you leave your cabin during the evening?"

"No I didn't. Early to bed, early to rise."

At that moment we were interrupted by the captain entering the sitting room. He came directly to our table.

"I hoped to find you here." Captain Harvey said. He handed me two telegrams. "The first two replies to your questions."

I opened them both. The first was regarding my query about Mr Marcus Bakerson. It confirmed that there was no current warrant out for him. I scribbled a quick reply to the telegram and returned it to the captain. The second was about Mr Roland Ashton. It confirmed that he was not known at his address. I folded the telegram with a frown and placed it in my pocket.

"I hoped Mr Heiss was here." Captain Harvey asked. "He has received a telegram also."

"He returned to his suite to change clothes." I said. "I had hoped to buy him a drink."

"I will deliver the telegram to him there."

I waited until the captain had left the sitting room before returning to my questions.

"Who do you think murdered Mr Herts?"

"It was the butler who did it." Imogen said. "Isn't he always the killer according to the Strand magazine?"

"In real life the butler never has a motive for killing someone." I said. "We look at those people that benefit the most from his death. Means, motive, and opportunity."

"Have you found anyone who has all three?" Imogen asked.

"Almost everyone."

Chapter Sixteen

I waved Roland into a seat.

We had remained in the sitting room watching the storm create havoc on the promenade deck. It was dark from the storm clouds. Mrs Colchester had joined us with her crochet.

Roland Ashton had changed his jacket since our adventure on the promenade deck. The jacket was shabby with patches on both the elbows and shoulders. Roland noticed me glancing at the patches.

"This is my lucky jacket." Roland said. "In the bush in New Zealand, when we were chasing a deer, my jacket was torn quite badly so I asked my manservant to patch it up. I did not want to ruin another jacket crawling through the mud. Since then it has served me well. I always seem to bag a trophy when I wear it."

"I hope you are not intending to bag a trophy today." I said with a laugh.

"There are no deer in New Zealand outside of zoos." Mrs Colchester said.

There was an uncomfortable silence for a moment. Roland paled.

"Obviously it was not New Zealand of which I am thinking." Roland said with a forced laugh. "I am always out and about, hunting in different continents."

"In fact, I am not sure if you have been to Africa from your descriptions." Mrs Colchester said.

"Please Mrs Colchester, don't tell all my secrets." Roland protested.

"Fortunately those are not secrets that are pertaining to this case." I said.

I nodded to Elisabeth to start a new page. She was staring at Roland. With a blush, she loaded some more ink into her fountain pen. I waited for her to finish before I began.

"Let us start with a little bit of background from you Mr Ashton." I said in a formal tone of voice. "Can you tell me sir, where are you from and what you do for a living?"

"A little bit of everything I suppose." Roland said. "I spend a lot of time hunting across the continents. I take people on safari. I give them a little adventure. I know a lot of the natives and can provide the necessary contacts."

"For a price."

"Of course for a price. A workman earns his wages."

"You do this anywhere in Africa?"

"Or Palestine, or South America." Roland said

"Do you speak any of the languages?" I asked.

"Why is that relevant?"

"It is relevant to me because it would perhaps be the first question that Mr Herts would ask you." I said. "It was for Mr Herts that you were putting on this show wasn't it? He is a known gun smuggler in Africa. Were you offering him your services? Offering to smuggle for him perhaps?"

"This is an outrageous accusation." Roland said.

"Gun smuggling is an outrageous act Mr Ashton." I said. "Did he refuse your services? Perhaps that made you angry. There is a lot of money to be made in gun smuggling."

"I know of Mr Herts but I have never met him before in my life." Roland Ashton said. "Nor do I condone gun smuggling. As I said I hunt animals in Africa, Palestine and South America."

"Yesterday you were saying that you hunted in Australia and New Zealand. Do you not hunt there any more?"

"Well I do, but I don't provide hunting services there."

I leaned back and crossed my legs. Roland Ashton stared at me defiantly, his roguish smile had disappeared. I did not think he was the killer, he did not have a motive and had disappeared from the sitting room quite early. But he was a liar, and not a very good one.

"Where do you live?" I asked.

"I have a small flat in London, on Pentecoat Lane." Roland Ashton said. "17B Pentecoat Lane. It is a small flat, but quite comfortable."

"That is the address that you gave to the airship company when you booked your ticket?" I asked.

"Yes."

"Then why are you unknown at that address?" I said. I produced the telegram I had received earlier from my pocket. "I sent a radiotelegraphy message enquiring about all the passengers on-board this airship. This telegram about you was one of the first to reply."

I opened the telegram slowly, my eyes never left Roland Ashton. He started to tease a thread on his jacket. It was an unconscious, nervous gesture. I read the telegram out loud.

"PERSON KNOWN AS ROLAND ASHTON NOT KNOWN AT THIS ADDRESS STOP ADDRESS IS A GREENGROCER SHOP WITH NO UPSTAIRS ACCESS END"

"Obviously there is a mistake." Roland Ashton said.

"Obviously." I said.

I tucked the telegram in my pocket again.

"As you can imagine. A murder investigation in which I do not know where a suspect is from, or what he does for a living, is difficult." I paused for a moment for effect. "It, in fact, makes the suspect look even more suspicious. If the suspect is lying about simple things like that, how much more is he likely to lie about his actions during the time of the murder?"

"That is easy. I was in bed at the time."

"Roland, Roland." I shook my head. "I have not established what time the murder took place."

I smiled. I had thrown him off-balance with that comment.

"But it was late last night. Everyone said the mysterious figure appeared in the corridors after midnight."

"But was that the killer?" I asked. "That could be related to something else. Perhaps that person happened to be in the wrong bedroom last night and was simply changing rooms. Which bedroom were you in last night?"

I ignored Elisabeth's flush.

"My own."

"All night?"

"I went to bed after nine o'clock, perhaps half past nine and stayed there until morning."

"How are you so sure of the time?"

"I have a pocket watch. I am sure of the time."

"And you were not the mysterious figure prowling the corridor?"

"No. I was not."

Roland was getting even more agitated. He did have secrets but were they relevant to the case? I hated secrets. I hated people lying to me, especially during an investigation. However I did not think he was guilty.

"Did you kill Mr Herts?"

Roland Ashton met my eyes before he answered with a curt 'No'.

"Earlier in the evening." I said. "Did you see anyone near Mrs Colchester's scissors or near her sewing basket?"

"I did not and, before you ask, I did not touch her sewing basket either."

"Who do you think killed Mr Herts?"

"You for all I know." Roland Ashton said. "Mr Bakerson probably. He was arguing with Herts during the evening, they seemed to be discussing something important. I overheard Mr Herts threaten Mr Bakerson earlier, perhaps Mr Bakerson wanted to get his revenge. Why have you not questioned Mr Bakerson yet?"

I consulted my list.

"Mr Bakerson is, in fact, next on my list of suspects to question." I said.

"Is that all?"

At my nod, he jumped to his feet and marched to the sitting room door. The door slammed behind him.

"So where is he from, if his address is all wrong?" Mrs Colchester asked.

"I have made further enquiries." I said. "There is more to Mr Ashton than meets the eye. Do you think he is the murderer?"

"I don't think he's the killer." Elisabeth said. I looked at her in surprise, I had forgotten she was still there. She blushed slightly. "He does not look the type. I mean, he does not seem to be the kind of man who would hurt a fly."

"You cannot judge a man by his appearance." Mrs Colchester said. Her voice was kind as she smiled at Elisabeth.

"He kills animals for a living." I said. "It is not that big a step to killing a man."

At that moment the door to the sitting room opened. Marcus Bakerson stood in the doorway. His normal angry scowl was absent.

"I think I killed Reginald Herts."

Chapter Seventeen

I raised an eyebrow.

I could smell strong alcohol from his breath but he did not appear to be drunk. I invited him to a chair and he walked across the sitting room and sat heavily in it. He stared back at me with his piggy eyes. I felt a wave of revulsion at his brutish appearance.

"You think you killed him?" I asked.

"I was the reason for his death." Marcus Bakerson said. "I have known Reginald Herts for several years now. I do delivery work for him."

"What sort of delivery work?"

"Nothing illegal." Bakerson said hurriedly. "I deliver things to him. Usually it is a message or perhaps it is a painting or some jewellery that he purchased through an auction. I bring it to his flat and he decides what to do with it. Sometimes he keeps them, sometimes he sells it on. Yesterday it was some documents that he … ahh … got through another auction. He had ordered me to deliver them to him. He was going to sell the documents in Rome."

I had a fair idea of what sort of 'auction' he meant. Reginald Herts was a receiver of stolen goods.

"What were the documents?"

"I don't know what they were. They were in a small, brown valise. They had drawings on them. It looked like a ship."

"Who gave the documents to you?"

"It was a contact. Herts had told me to expect the delivery and bring them to him. He did not say who he was."

"Did anyone else know you had the documents?"

"I didn't tell no one." Bakerson said. "But Herts did inform people that he was going to have an auction in Rome so people would have known that he had them."

"How much was he selling them for?"

"The bidding was to start at ten thousand pounds."

My mouth dropped open. Mrs Colchester gasped. I could hear the scratching of the pen had stopped as well. Ten thousand pounds was a fortune. You could buy half of London for that sort of money.

"That is why you think you were the reason for his death?" I managed to ask. I was still astounded by the amount.

"I think the documents were military plans for the new Dreadnought line of battleships that England is building." Bakerson said. "Mr Herts was selling them to the Germans. I think the German diplomat, Kurt Heiss, is the man who murdered Mr Herts. He murdered him to get the plans for the Dreadnoughts."

I thought for a moment. It was certainly a strong motive for murder.

"Why would he kill Mr Herts now?" I asked. "Would it not be easier for him to follow Mr Herts to Rome and attend the auction?"

"Perhaps he did not want to pay the ten thousand pounds." Bakerson said.

"The brown valise was empty." I said. "I did not see any documents in the room when I searched it, which means that is the likely motive for the killing. The killer has already got them."

"It was definitely the Germans." Bakerson said. "They did it."

"You also had a motive." I said. "You knew the documents were there. You knew the value of them. Perhaps you changed your mind and decided to keep the documents for yourself."

"No, it wasn't me." Bakerson said. "I'm just the delivery man. I collect the items and delivery them."

"You had an argument with Mr Herts earlier in the evening." I said. "What was the argument about?"

"It was nothing really. We were just discussing politics, as men do. Just trying to decide the politics of the government, which politics are the best."

Even to my ears, this explanation sounded patently false.

"One last job Mr Herts had said. You had promised him one last job, what job was that?"

"Delivery job. He wanted me for one more delivery job. Nothing unusual about that."

"Delivery job? After that you were retiring?"

I could see that Bakerson's jaw was set in a stubborn line. I was not going to get a better explanation from him. I tried a different tack.

"Tell me about last night. You had an argument with Roland Ashton."

"Him? He's a right twerp. Since I first met him, he's been trying to worm his way into Herts's operations. Trying to get into his good graces, so he could help sell guns in Africa."

"I thought he did not know Mr Herts." Elisabeth said, interrupting us.

"Told you that, did he?" Bakerson laughed. An ugly sound. "He's outright lying, he is. You would not believe his innocent face but he was always snooping around Mr Herts, trying to get his foot in the door."

"I don't believe you." Elisabeth said.

"I don't care if you do Missy." Bakerson leaned forward with a suggestive leer. "Though if it's something that you want to discuss later perhaps?"

"Back to the matter at hand, Mr Bakerson." I said. I slammed my hand on the arm of the sofa. Elisabeth jumped slightly but Bakerson simply leaned back in his chair.

"Yeah well, don't you go believing Ashton. Whatever he said about me, it isn't true."

"What might he have said about you?" I asked.

"Nothing at all."

I looked down at my notes. The telegram I had received earlier about Bakerson had said that he was not currently under a warrant, so I had nothing but my own suspicions.

"Did you kill Reginald Herts?"

"Here we go." Bakerson said. "I bring you news about the reason he died. A clue, mind you as well, and I'm accused of murdering him. Typical."

"It's a simple question, did you kill him?"

"Well here's a simple answer. No, I bloody well did not."

"Were you near the sewing basket at any time during the evening?"

"No, and I didn't touch no scissors neither."

"Who do you think killed him?"

"Kurt Heiss obviously, him and his lady wife."

"Just because they're German?"

"There's a war on its way between us and the Germans." Bakerson said. "Do you really think they would hesitate for a second to kill us if it would give them an advantage. Those were plans for a warship. He's a killer all right."

"Could anyone else have killed him?"

"Simon Charles could have. He's a lawyer and all. His wife is no angel either. I knew her when I was growing up in London. She's a cold fish."

I tried to picture Simon Charles as a killer. Dressed in his funeral suit, grey face and intense blue eyes. Or perhaps his wife with the dazzling smile. I shook my head. Bakerson was playing with me. I could see it from the expression on his brutish face. There was a half smile on his lips.

"Well thank you Mr Bakerson." I said. "I'll get back to you if I have any further questions."

I watched Bakerson heave himself to his feet. There was a distant rumble of thunder as he walked towards the door. A portent of danger I was sure. He stopped at the door and looked back at me.

"Reginald Herts was no choirboy." Bakerson said. "Do you ever think that the world might be a better place without him in it?"

He disappeared through the door. I looked after him. The uncharitable thought sprang in my head that the world would be a better place without someone like Marcus Bakerson as well.

Chapter Eighteen

I changed for afternoon tea and joined my cousins Imogen and Elisabeth.

Elisabeth looked stunning in a cream dress. Her red hair hung over her shoulder, tied up with a black velvet band. Imogen had changed to a different pair of shoes (I do notice these things sometimes) and added a matching resin brooch. I put on my jacket. Sometimes, us men get it so easy.

Afternoon tea was delicious. The chef had created a delightful steamed pudding to die for. Imogen ordered a pot of tea for us in the sitting room.

Almost everyone was there.

Kurt and Dorothy Heiss retired to their suite within minutes of entering the sitting room as anti-German sentiment made it uncomfortable for them. Simon Charles seemed to be the most vocal against them. I stood and raised my hands.

"Ladies and gentlemen."

I waited for a moment for the hubbub to die down.

"Ladies and gentlemen. It is not in my nature to comment on an ongoing investigation however I am quite distraught at the comments against our two German fellow passengers. They are suspects in the murder -" I had to raise my voice at this point as the hub bub started again, "but so are you. It is quite unwarranted to place blame where there is none, and the investigation has not concluded."

I sat down again.

"That has put the cat among the pigeons." Elisabeth said. "Mr Bakerson is giving you quite the glare."

"Elisabeth." Imogen said. There was a warning tone in her voice.

"Well, he is." Elisabeth said. She subsided in her chair.

"May we join you?" A voice said.

I looked up, Lord Vellance and his wife stood next to my chair. I stood and offered them both a chair and they sat gratefully.

"Simon Charles has started a betting ring on who you will arrest." Lord Vellance said.

"Who are the favourites?" I asked.

"Kurt Heiss is the favourite, Marcus Bakerson and Mrs Colchester are in the running however."

"You are here to get the inside scoop?"

"I am here because I am worried about our reputation." Lord Vellance said. "I am worried that the slightest taint on us, from this investigation, will do untold damage. I want to know how the investigation is going."

I shook my head.

"Obviously I would like to help you." I said. "But unless I can confirm who the killer is, everyone will remain a suspect. We will not return to London until tomorrow, so I still have time to investigate."

"Perhaps we can help you then." Lady Vellance said.

"How can you do that?"

"You discussed the Case of the Missing Cat yesterday evening in the smoking room. You allowed the passengers to pick holes in the case and come up with ideas. Perhaps you can do the same here. I mean, how hard can it be?"

I thought for a second. There was some merit in her idea. I did need help in coming up with ideas.

The podium was dragged from the smoking room into the sitting room. I asked for it to be placed near the clockwork smoke extractor fan which blessedly sucked the cigar smoke from the room. With my back to the double glass doors leading to the promenade deck and, with the occasional lightening flash brightening the room, I engaged with my audience.

"Lady Vellance has kindly suggested that discussing the death of Mr Herts with you might be helpful in generating ideas about the murder." I said. "Can we think for a second about how the murder was committed. There is no such thing as a stupid idea so, any suggestion would be appreciated. How did the murderer get into the suite of Mr Herts without anyone noticing him and kill the man without him raising an outcry?"

There was a silence after my question and I took the moment to take a sip from the glass of water the steward had kindly provided me. Then Elisabeth raised her hand.

"Was it a murder? Could it have been a suicide? Could Mr Herts have decided in his drunken state to end it all?"

"That's an interesting question. Doctor, I can see you hiding at the back, what do you think?"

Doctor Peters was indeed hiding at the back. The chairs had been arranged in a semi-circle of three rows and the doctor, the captain and a couple of the stewards had slipped in.

The doctor stood up, settled his thumb into a pocket of his waistcoat, and puffed out his chest.

"It could indeed have been suicide. The angle was directly into the centre of his chest and he certainly is strong enough to have punctured his ribs with the sharp scissors. I would not rule that explanation out."

"Or perhaps an accident." Elisabeth said again. "It was very stormy last night. If he was holding the scissors and tripped over in the storm, he could have stabbed himself."

"It can't have been suicide." Simon Charles had jumped to his feet. He looked even more like a funeral director in the setting with the rows of seats surrounding the pulpit. "Why would he have stolen Mrs Colchesters' scissors if he wanted to commit suicide? Why would he have that damn German's pipe in his hand if he committed suicide?"

There was a murmur around the room. I could clearly hear the name Heiss.

"An additional point would be that some documents belonging to Mr Herts are missing, presumably stolen by the murderer." I said. "That suggests at the very least that he had someone else in his room at the time of his death."

There were thoughtful nods around the room and whispered conversations as people quickly discussed the implications of this tasty gossip.

"I suggest that suicide can be ruled out therefore, does everyone agree?"

There was a consensus of nods around the room.

"Elisabeth, can you take a note please." I said. "So how could a murderer have managed to enter the room without Mr Herts making a scene?"

"Perhaps he did not." Roland Ashton stood for a moment. "The porthole was open. I have seen in circuses where the clowns have thrown knives at moving targets. Could someone have lowered themselves down the outside of the airship and thrown the pair of scissors through the porthole, then winched themselves away?"

"For that matter, I have seen knife throwing artefacts in the British Museum." Lord Vellance said. "I'm sure that someone clever could adapt it for a pair of scissors."

"That is possible." I said. "It does not explain how the documents are missing nor why Mr Heiss's pipe was found in his hand."

"Perhaps he never had the documents in the first place and, as for the pipe, he could have found the pipe and was in the process of returning the pipe to Mr Heiss."

"Why not suggest that the murderer turned himself invisible?" Simon Charles said. "That's just as good an explanation."

"I have examined the porthole from the outside." I said. "It required a second person on the winch to lower me down and lift me back up. It was not very stable either, I was spinning around with every gust. It would be impossible for someone to throw or shoot a pair of scissors accurately. I suggest that it is not a very good explanation either."

"So you think that the killer waited for an opportune moment and simply walked in and killed him?" Captain Harvey stood. "He would have been very brave to do that with the steward in the corridor."

"Someone could have dressed like him and the steward would only have seen the back of him. The steward would not have realised that it was someone else."

"Perhaps the killer waited until there was a lot of chaos in the corridor and slipped into the room."

"The murderer could have hid in the room earlier when the steward was not looking, waited until Mr Herts returned, and killed him then."

"It sounds like we have a few reasonable explanations." I said. "So we have a way for the murderer to have got into the room undetected, and without turning invisible." That last comment I directed towards Simon Charles who frowned at me. "He managed to kill Mr Herts quietly, either because he surprised Mr Herts, or because he was expected in the room by Mr Herts. Then he escaped. How did he escape?"

"I thought you had established that the mysterious figure was the murderer?" April Fabersham said. "The murderer had bundled himself up in a heavy coat and escaped in his disguise while the steward was otherwise engaged."

"That is the assumption that I am making but, may I remind everyone, it is merely an assumption." I said. It had been hammered into me so many times over the years by my sergeant about the inadvisability of making 'stupid-ass assumptions'. His words, not mine. "I want to explore other possibilities."

"He could have left by the large window." Elisabeth said.

"Only the porthole was open." Simon Charles said.

"Yes but, if he tied a string on the window latch and fed it through the porthole, he could have climbed out of the large window, across to the porthole and closed the big window from outside the porthole after he climbed out and pulled the string free afterwards."

"That is possible." I said slowly. I did not want to upset Elisabeth. Occam's razor. The easiest explanations were usually the most likely. "We can examine the window latch afterwards and see if there is any wear on it indicating a piece of string was involved."

"I still think that it was this mysterious figure that did it. If it wasn't him, why has he not come forward?" Mrs Colchester said.

"Perhaps the last person to speak to Herts alive was the person that stabbed him." Roland Ashton said. "Then pretended a conversation with him to confuse onlookers. You were last to see him Mr Charles, is that how you killed him?"

A flicker of consternation fled across Simon Charles's face and I suppressed a bitter laugh. Simon Charles was so eager to blame everyone else, it was satisfying to see his reaction when he was blamed for something. Edith Charles clutched his hand, her dazzling smile was missing.

"Another alternative is, if the murderer did not leave the room." I said. Everyone's attention snapped to me. "After killing Mr Herts they could have hidden in the room. Although we searched the room, we did not, for example, search the wardrobe. It has a shoe shelf at the bottom which is large enough for a man to hide underneath."

There was a few moments of silence while people thought about this.

"You mean that he was there all the time?" Lady Vellance looked like she was about to faint.

"For that matter, he could have hid behind the door and joined the crowd at the door when they ran to investigate the screams." I said.

"That's outrageous." Edmund Potts said.

"It's also impossible." Roland Ashton said. "The steward and I were the first at the scene. There was no one behind the door when we arrived."

"No one that you saw." I said.

"No one at all." Roland Ashton said. His normally handsome smile was set in a line. His right hand clenched and unclenched.

"There is another possibility that has occurred to me." I said. "If Mr Herts was not dead but merely in a faint, then the first person to approach the body might have taken the opportunity to stab him while he was helpless. Do you think that is possible Mr Ashton?"

"I was not the first through the door, the maid and steward were before me." Roland Ashton said.

"That is correct, however the maid fainted, and the steward ran for the doctor. Did you stab Mr Herts while their backs were turned?"

Roland Ashton stood up abruptly. Every eye in the room was fixed upon him and, for a moment, I thought he was going to throw himself at me. Instead he took a deep calming breath.

"I resent your accusations Detective Sergeant." Roland Ashton said. He walked to the door, his heels stabbing into the carpet of the sitting room. "I will not remain to hear any further baseless accusations."

The door thudded closed after him. I felt a little sorry for him. Although Mr Herts's body was still warm when I found him, I felt the rigidity in his muscles which suggested that he was long dead. However I took umbrage at the lies Roland Ashton told me earlier.

I stepped down from the small podium and indicated to the stewards to remove it. The passengers stood and broke into small groups discussing the events in soft tones. My cousins Imogen and Elisabeth both joined me.

"Do you really think that he did it, that he killed Mr Herts?" Elisabeth asked. She was breathless for some reason.

"Roland Ashton? He had the means as most of us did." I said. "The scissors were easy to obtain from the sewing basket and he was present here for part of the evening. The motive I am not sure about. He has told me lies about knowing Mr Herts which makes me think that he has something to hide. The opportunity? Perhaps he was the mysterious figure."

"Why did you say that the mysterious figure was not the killer?"

"I did not say that. I wanted to explore other possibilities, and I also wanted to distract everyone. I wanted to study the faces of the passengers when I revealed that the mysterious figure might not be the killer. It was curious."

"What did their faces reveal?"

"Most of them were confused." I paused for a moment. "The steward's face showed relief, perhaps he felt guilty for not stopping the passenger or asking his identity. Marcus Bakerson's face looked thoughtful. I would wager that he is not as stupid as his brutish countenance would suggest. Edith Charles's face looked relieved, but I do not know why it would. It is interesting to study peoples' reactions, but it is not always revealing and certainly is not something I could take to a court."

"Perhaps Edith Charles looked relieved because the idea of a mysterious killer stalking the corridor at night is more scary to her than a killer hiding in a crowd in daylight." Imogen said.

I nodded dubiously. Perhaps.

Chapter Nineteen

Mrs April Fabersham was the last passenger on my list to interview.

She was quite petite and very attractive in a mousey way. She quietly joined us in the sitting room at a corner table, folding herself gracefully into a chair. Elisabeth sat next to her, her pink writing paper ready on the table. They were of the same height and build but that's where the similarity ended. Elisabeth had fiery red hair, tied up in an untidy wavy bundle. April Fabersham had sleek dark hair. Elisabeth was wearing a daring green dress, fashionable among the young ladies. April Fabersham was dressed demurely in a red silk dress.

April Fabersham confirmed that she was travelling to join her husband George in Rome. He was a senior broker for a major London Insurance company and was obliged to visit Rome on behalf of his employers. They had married recently and this would be their honeymoon together.

"Have you met Mr Herts in the past?" I asked.

"I've never met 'im nor 'eard of 'im." Mrs Fabersham said.

I frowned slightly at her accent.

"This is your first time on an airship." I said. "In fact, I would suggest that this is your first time outside of London?"

"That's right sir, 'ow did you know?"

"It is your accent. It is very unusual to hear your accent outside of London."

It was true. She sounded like a commoner. The more I thought about it the more it made sense. Marcus Bakerson said he knew her from when he was young so she must have been born near him in south London. Her husband did not invite her on the business trip but instead invited her to join him for a honeymoon afterwards. It suggested to me that he was embarrassed by her accent and mannerisms and did not want his colleagues to know he had married below his social circle.

"Well. Let us examine the events of yesterday. Can you tell me what you remember of yesterday evening?"

"Well sir we 'ad a lovely dinner and afterwards we sat 'ere in the sitting room for a big old chat." April Fabersham said.

"You sat over near the door didn't you?" I asked.

A flash of lightening lit up the room casting scary shadows across the wall. Mrs Fabersham jumped nervously. I resisted the urge to pat her hand.

"Not at first. At first I sat with Mrs Colchester and watched her knitting but I really got a bit bored I can tell you. After that Roland, I mean Mr Ashton, wanted to talk so 'e invited me for a glass of wine on a seat near the door. 'e was a right laugh 'e was, 'e thinks 'e is so smooth and sophisticated. Mr Bakerson came over to make a joke and it got right under 'is skin."

"Mr Bakerson mentioned that he knew you as a child."

"Marcus, yeah we used to run about together, peas-in-a-pod we were. I was right surprised when I saw 'im onboard."

"Where did you go then?"

"I was very embarrassed. Marcus can be crude sometimes. Mr Ashton escorted me back to the dining room where we sat for some time drinking wine. 'e entertained me with some fanciful stories about his 'unting expeditions. I'm not sure what time we sat until. I went to bed to read and 'e returned to the sitting room."

"Did you see anyone near Mrs Colchester's sewing basket or with Mrs Colchesters' scissors?"

"No sir."

"Did you leave your cabin at any time last night?"

"No sir."

"Did you see anything suspicious or hear anything suspicious during the night? Anything at all, regardless of how small or harmless?"

She shook her head.

I regarded her for a moment. I know it is wrong for me to judge a person by their appearance but, to me, she looked innocent. She looked at me through guileless eyes, her expression was concerned but not worried.

"Who do you think killed Mr Herts?" I asked.

A rumble of thunder interrupted us followed immediately by a bright flash of lightening. The storm was on top of us. I could hear the muted cadence of rain drops attacking the windows.

"I know who didn't, and that was Marcus Bakerson." April Fabersham said. "People will look at 'im and automatically judge 'im as guilty just because of 'is brutish appearance. Mark my words, 'e has an innocent soul. People do not look past 'is broken nose. They do not consider that 'e might be innocent."

"Thank you Mrs Fabersham." I smiled, letting my voice soften. "I am grateful for you reminding me of that."

I stood politely and waited until April Fabersham left the table. She stopped and looked around her uncertainly for a few moments before crossing the room to join Mrs Potts and Mrs Colchester at the sitting room window. They split apart to allow Mrs Fabersham to sit between them. Then shared a laugh while watching the storm. A shadow crossed the window. A deckhand perhaps?

Even now I remember that scene with horror. The three ladies with their heads together gaily laughing and enjoying the dance of lightening across the sky from the safety of their chairs.

That's when the lights went out and the screaming started.

Chapter Twenty

The darkness was total.

There was a loud rumble of thunder and another flash of lightening outside. The room lit up. I grabbed Elisabeth's hand and pulled her closer to me, my right arm sheltering her shoulders. I could hear Marcus Bakerson's voice as he shouted for the stewards to bring some lights. There were vague shadows in the dark room fumbling blindly for the door.

I groped for Imogen's hand and held it tight.

"Both of you ladies remain here." I said.

I rummaged in my pocket for my cigar lighter. My flame was a solitary light in the chaos and drew people towards it. With the light in my eyes the darkness beyond was absolute. Mr Potts was the first to appear in the gloom. I gave a start. For a moment his head seemed disembodied in the darkness.

"Victoria?" Mr Potts called.

"I am here," was the reply. "Quite safe with Mrs Colchester and Mrs Fabersham. We are holding each other's hands."

"I can help." Elisabeth said.

"You can help by staying here with your Aunt Imogen." I said. "The storm has probably knocked the steam engine offline. Or perhaps the electric lines between the steam engine and here have failed. I do have a bad feeling about this."

"When I was young, we had a big store of candles." Mr Potts said. "None of this modern steam technology like we have today."

"Let us hope that the stewards have the presence of mind to bring those wind up lights from the bedrooms to here." I said. I raised my voice louder to call out. "Is everyone all right?"

A chorus of affirmative voices replied to my question.

A second cigar lighter was ignited. A bluish glow in the dark. I could see it belonged to Lord Vellance. He was standing next to the sitting room door. He held his wife's hand, by her expression perhaps too tightly.

"Everyone stay where they are." I said. "I do not want you to trip and fall in the darkness. Lord Vellance, you are next to the door, can you call for a steward?"

"Perhaps ask him to arrange for a pot of tea for everyone. It does calm you down marvellously." Mrs Colchester said.

"Order me a large brandy instead." Marcus Bakerson's voice joined in, out of the gloom. "I don't do pots of tea. Unless it's a large tea with some brandy in it. That would suit me fine."

Lord Vellance opened the door and stepped through into the corridor. His backlit figure disappeared as the door closed behind him.

"Does anyone else have a cigar lighter?" I asked.

"I regret to say that I left mine in the smoking room." Mr Potts said. "Perhaps we can all move there and search for other lights?"

"No." I said. "Lord Vellance and the steward should be returning momentarily. In fact I will move to the door and see what is taking them so long."

"Don't go, please don't leave us." I identified the voice as belonging to Lady Vellance.

"I am not leaving." I assured her through gritted teeth. I had accidentally kicked over a low table in the darkness, clipping my shins in the process.

I stumbled again, this time over someone's feet, as I made my way to the door. I did not identify his or her voice as we mutually apologised for my clumsiness. I reached the door just as it swung open. Lord Vellance was holding a clockwork light taken from the bedroom area. He was followed closely by the steward.

I recognised the steward from the bedroom corridor. He carried several clockwork lights which he thrust into my open hands. Only one was lit and I hooked it on the wall next to the door. The other three clockwork lights I hurriedly wound the mechanism before passing them to Lord Vellance to distribute.

"What happened to -" I stopped, the steward had disappeared.

"Do we know what happened to the main electrical lights?" I asked Lord Vellance.

Lord Vellance replied with a shrug.

"The steward says he thinks we were struck by lightening. The surge of power must have overloaded the circuit breakers and tripped a fuse. We are very lucky that the balloon is filled with helium instead of hydrogen."

"Did he say when power will be restored?" I asked.

I had a spare light, so I placed it on the table in front of Imogen and Elisabeth. The pale glow illuminated their frightened expressions.

"I forgot to ask." Lord Vellance said. "The steward will return soon. He is collecting a few more lights to place in the smoking room."

"All we need is a pianoforte and we could have a right good sing-a-long." Mr Potts said.

"Do you play?" I asked.

"When I was younger and my fingers were more nimble." Mr Potts replied. "Victoria was a good singer. She had the voice of an angel when she was eighteen. She cannot hold a note now that she is getting hard of hearing unfortunately."

I tried and failed to picture Mrs Potts as an eighteen year old.

"I enjoyed singing when I was younger." I said. "I sang in a choir. I had the highest voice in the parish, the sweetest voice you would ever hear."

"And then your voice dropped?" Mr Potts asked.

"And then my voice dropped." I confirmed. "You have been together with Mrs Potts since you were eighteen?"

"I met her when we were both eighteen." Mr Potts said. "I proposed to her when we were nineteen. I had to propose to her three times before she would accept."

"She was picky."

"Yes, but she had good taste in the end."

I laughed. It felt strange to laugh in the eerie darkness. The thunder and lightening still rolled and flashed outside.

The electric light flickered slightly then returned bright, as if it had never disappeared. I felt my shoulders relax. I hated the darkness. I had too many bad memories of chasing machete-wielding religious crazies across rooftops on moonless nights. But that is another story.

A loud cheer went around the room.

Lord Vellance had rejoined his wife. I don't think they realised it but they were holding hands again. Mrs Colchester had fallen over in the darkness and Mrs Potts was helping her stand. Strangely Mrs

Fabersham had not stirred from her seat. Marcus Bakerson sat back with his feet on a table. He had somehow obtained a bottle of wine which he was drinking direct from the neck of the bottle.

I was about to cross to him and remonstrate with him but the image of him drinking from the bottle without any glasses gave me pause. The bottle in Mr Herts's room did not have any accompanying glasses. Was Bakerson the mysterious stranger. Perhaps he had joined Mr Herts for a last drink in his room and had murdered him for the documents. By his own admission, he was the only person who had knowledge of the worth of those documents.

"… it still does not excuse his boorish behaviour."

I turned, startled. Imogen had appeared beside me without my noticing her. Part of my mind wondered, how does she do that?

"I beg your pardon."

"I said, he might have had a fright but he is still boorish." Imogen said.

"You mean Mr Bakerson?"

"I saw you staring at him. I thought for a second that you were going to approach him and give him a telling off."

I was saved from a reply by a question from Mrs Potts.

"I wonder what this is?"

She was looking at a hole in the window near her chair. A spiderweb of cracks radiated out from the centre of the hole.

"I wonder if the lightening had caused this. Perhaps we had a lightening strike."

I had a feeling of cold dread in the pit of my stomach as I recognised it. It was a bullet hole.

"Stand back." I said in an authoritative voice.

I joined Mrs Potts and Mrs Colchester at the window and politely ushered them out of the way. The bullet hole was at about waist level. I followed the path the bullet must have taken. Mrs April Fabersham was still sitting in the middle seat at the table, smiling blankly in front of her. Her demure, red dress had a small hole above her heart. A red stain, darker than the silk dress, covered her chest and stomach.

That's when the screaming started.

Chapter Twenty-One

With a thunder of footsteps, the door to the sitting room burst open. One of the stewards and several of the passengers crowded through the doorway.

"Get the doctor." I shouted.

But I had seen death too many times not to recognise its appointment. I had spoken to April Fabersham less than ten minutes before she was murdered. I had been charmed by her innocence. A commoner like me. Someone who had transported herself from the gutter. She had felt out of place among a different social circle, trapped by her accent, but she had tried her best.

The men still stood at the entrance of the sitting room.

"A doctor." I all but screamed.

One of them peeled off.

"Dammit to Hades." I whispered.

I felt the tears prickling at the corners of my eyes and blinked them back with an effort. This investigation was not over and I was damned if I was going to let them see me cry.

One of the men approached.

"No, stay out. Someone in this room has shot Mrs Fabersham and I am going to find out whom it was."

There was a moment of stunned silence. I stood and looked about. The only people who had been present in the room were: Lord and Lady Vellance; Marcus Bakerson; Mr and Mrs Potts; Mrs Colchester; and my cousins Imogen and Elisabeth. I ushered the others from the room.

Simon Charles returned with the doctor. Part of me noted with amusement how silly Simon Charles looked trying to run in a pair of ill-fitting bedroom slippers.

Doctor Peters confirmed the time of death. I asked Elisabeth to make a note.

"She was laughing when she was shot." Doctor Peters said. "She did not feel a thing."

"Just at the moment the lights went out there was a flash of lightening and a rumble of thunder." I said. "The killer took that opportunity to kill Mrs Fabersham."

"Why did he do that?" Imogen asked.

"Let me find the killer first, then I can ask him." I said. "I want everyone to return to where they were standing or sitting at the time that the lights went out."

I helped Imogen and Elisabeth right the table which I had knocked over in my rush to the door earlier. I looked around. Only Bakerson had not moved. He was standing next to the dead body of Mrs Fabersham, looking at her with a bewildered expression on his face.

"Bakerson." I snapped.

He said nothing, just looked at me with a mute appeal in his face. My heels dug into the soft carpet as I strode across to him.

"Get back to your place." I said in a harsh whisper.

I stared at him until he backed down. I waited until he returned to a seat. The bottle of wine remained on the table and he grabbed it, drinking deeply.

The doctor had not moved Mrs Fabersham's body. He looked at me and shook his head. Mrs Potts and Mrs Colchester refused to return to their positions next to the dead body, and I did not have the heart to order them.

I lined myself up behind Mrs Fabersham until her body was in the way of the bullet hole. Then I looked behind me – at Bakerson.

I walked over to Bakerson. He followed me with his eyes as I knelt next to his table comparing the line from Bakerson to Mrs Fabersham then to the bullet hole. It was not perfect, but it was close enough. Lord and Lady Vellance watched me, puzzled.

I gave Bakerson a smile that was not a smile as I dropped into a chair next to him. I extracted a cigar from my pocket. He was glaring at me as I lit it.

"So, Mr Marcus Bakerson." I said. I puffed out some smoke, quite rudely, in his direction. "Tell me, why did you kill Mrs Fabersham."

He started and stared around wildly. His brutish face turned a deep red as he stood up.

"I ought to mash you for saying that." Bakerson said. "I loved her, I did. She was my bestest friend in the whole wide world."

He towered over me. I leaned back on my chair and said nothing.

"What makes you think I killed her anyway. I was sitting over here when she got herself shot. I didn't do nothing."

"You were sitting here." I said. "You shot her from here, the bullet went through her and through the window beyond her."

I made a gun with my fingers and played out the scene as I imagined how he did it, even making a childish popping noise. I looked at his face. The colour of his face had changed from a reddish hue to almost purple. He made a strangled noise and swung a huge fist at my head.

At one time in my distant youth, I was the boxing champion at my school in Roath, Cardiff. I had not continued through to the regional finals due to injury but I always fancied that I would have taken at least a silver in my weight class. That helped me with his first punch.

I ducked his wild hay-maker punch with ease but I found myself entangled in the chair as his second punch sought my face. I threw myself backwards, landing on the carpet with a soft thump. I rolled to my feet, my hands already clenched into fists.

"Stop this now." Imogen shouted in her imperious voice.

I hesitated.

Bakerson threw a roundhouse punch to my chin. I stepped inside it. Once. Twice. Thrice. My third punch laid him out on the ground. His broken nose was leaking blood.

My blood was up.

I wanted to stamp on his head and squash him like a bug. The last few months of chasing killers through the streets of London had taught me one thing, and that was not to give any quarter. But there were witnesses here to stop me. I could not give vent to my fears and anger.

I looked around. Elisabeth looked at me in fascination. Imogen was horror-stricken. Lady Vellance had fainted. Mrs Colchester and Mrs Potts were made of sterner stuff and approached me.

"That is quite enough young man." Mrs Colchester said.

I nodded and turned away. I opened the door to the sitting room. The captain was waiting patiently outside.

"Do you have an appropriate cell where we can place Mr Bakerson under arrest?"

The Captain thought for a moment.

"We do have a store room in the balloon above. We can empty it and lock the door, he will be quite secure there."

"That would be perfect, thank you."

I stepped aside to allow a couple of burly stewards to enter the sitting room. They lifted Bakerson and started to drag him from the room.

"Wait." Doctor Peters called.

I motioned to the stewards to stop and they halted at the entrance eyeing me curiously. I crossed to the doctor. He motioned to Mrs Fabersham's body.

"What is it?" I asked.

"The bullet did not penetrate through the body." Doctor Peters said.

"So, what of it?"

"If Mr Bakerson had shot the bullet, there is no way it could have hit Mrs Fabersham and also gone through the window." Doctor Peters said. "The only way this could have happened ..."

"Is if it was shot from outside into the room." I completed Doctor Peters's sentence.

"Does that mean that Mr Bakerson is innocent?" Captain Harvey asked.

"Yes." I said. "It means that everyone in this room was innocent of this murder. The killer was one of the passengers outside."

Chapter Twenty-Two

The same stretcher that was used to take Mr Herts's body was employed to lift Mrs Fabersham's body. The stewards also took the blood soaked cushions, that she had been sitting on, away with them.

Mr Bakerson was still unconscious. By mutual consent he was carried by a pair of stewards to his cabin where the doctor attended him. I felt a little guilty about hitting him. He had swung the first punch but I was the more experienced fighter. I had put too much of my anger into my punches.

Elisabeth attended to my fists. The skin was broken, a sign that I was out of practice.

"Where did you learn to punch like that?" Imogen asked.

"I learnt when I was young on the streets of Cardiff." I said. "One of the teachers at my school encouraged me to practice and I became quite good at it."

"Did you have to hit him so hard?"

"What is the point of hitting him softly? Besides, he swung the first punch."

"Yes, but you are supposed to represent the law." Imogen said.

I shook my head.

"People like Bakerson do not recognise the law. Rightly or wrongly they do not believe in the need for law and order."

"He was innocent but you were about to lock him up."

"Until we return to London, I am the law." I paused, then pleaded to Imogen. "I have to be the law, don't you see? Otherwise law and order will break down."

Imogen nodded curtly to me then left without a word.

I nodded thanks to Elisabeth. She had placed some tape over my knuckles to hold the skin together.

"She is very frightened." Elisabeth said. "She doesn't mean what she said. Mrs Fabersham dying in front of her has scared her."

"Why are you are not frightened?" I asked.

"I'm a little bit. It was so sudden, I mean. One moment she was laughing, full of life, then the next moment she was gone. But mostly I'm glad that it wasn't me that died. I feel guilty. Guilty for being alive, guilty that she died instead of me. Is that wrong?"

The stewards returned with new pillows for the chair. I led Elisabeth back to the table in the corner.

"My mother would tell me to thank the Lord that I have survived." I said. "Perhaps that is the best advice I can give you. You were not responsible for the murder so, when you pray tonight, say a prayer for Mrs Fabersham's soul and a thank you to Him for surviving another day."

"Is that what you do?"

"I'm always glad to survive another day." I reached for Elisabeth's fold of pink paper and placed it on the table. "We need to do some work. We need to go through Mrs Fabersham's statement and see if there is anything in what she has told us which explains why she was targeted for murder."

Elisabeth quickly riffled through her notes until she found Mrs Fabersham's interview.

"She says that she did not know Mr Herts. She sat with Mrs Colchester until she got bored with the knitting then chatted with Mr

Ashton until Mr Bakerson interrupted. Then she went to the dining room with Mr Ashton. Then went to bed."

I shook my head bewildered.

"There is nothing in her statement that would point the finger at anyone." I said. "No reason to murder her."

"Perhaps the murderer thought that she had seen something or knew something."

"I think I need to speak to Mr Bakerson again." I said. "He seems to be the only connection between the two murder victims. He worked for Mr Herts and was best friends with Mrs Fabersham."

"Could it be the missing documents?" Elisabeth asked. "What if the killer could not find the documents and decided that Mr Bakerson had given them to Mrs Fabersham instead of to Mr Herts?"

"If that was the case then, why didn't the murderer kill Mr Bakerson?"

"Perhaps Mr Bakerson is the next person on the list."

"I think we need to question Mr Bakerson." I said. "We might start by searching his room and Mrs Fabersham's room."

Bakerson was awake when I started to search his room. He glared at me through his piggy eyes, a handkerchief pressed against his bloody nose. I was glad the stewards were there to restrain him just in case.

The room was smaller than mine. It had a similar wire bed in one corner. I took a cursory glance under the bed and confirmed only his walking boots and cane were there. The bedside table had an old fashioned pocket watch on top of it. A single drawer graced the front of the bedside table. I pulled at the handle and the bedside table fell forward, catching me unaware. The two stewards jumped slightly as the table boomed, the pocket watch skittered across the floor.

"I swear by the Gods that if you have broken my pocket watch, I will skin you alive."

I believed him. I retrieved the watch, placing it carefully on the table. The table was empty. His wardrobe contained only his clothes. I was impressed that he had brought a dinner jacket.

Elisabeth helped me in Mrs Fabersham's room. I smelled an almost imperceptible scent of rose perfume from the room. The kind that you try to inhale deeply to smell it better then realise it is gone and wonder did you imagine the smell.

The small drawer by the bed contained her night clothes and personal things. I let Elisabeth search through them. The wardrobe contained several dresses and a surprisingly large selection of shoes. I mentioned this to Elisabeth but she did not think this was suspicious.

Her bags were equally uninteresting. Although Elisabeth did get excited at Mrs Fabersham's selection of books. I returned to Mr Bakerson's room.

"So, Mr Herts is dead and now Mrs Fabersham." I said. "The only connection between the two of the murdered victims is you Mr Bakerson. Why is that?"

"I don't know nothing." Bakerson said.

"You told me that you had given the documents to Mr Herts. Did you actually give them to him, or did you hide them away?"

"I gave them to 'im all right."

"Or perhaps to Mrs Fabersham. Was she your co-conspirator? Was that why she was killed?"

He pushed himself into a sitting position. His face clouded with anger. One of the stewards took a step forward but I waved him back.

"She was just a friend. Look, she had nothing to do with this."

I sighed and sat in the rattan chair. Then continued in a calmer voice.

"You can surely see it from my point of view. You were to deliver a valuable document to Mr Herts. You then had an argument with him. He turns up dead. You are friends with Mrs Fabersham. You had an argument with Mr Ashton. She turns up dead. The documents, which by your own admission are worth ten thousand pounds, are missing."

Bakerson was looking resolutely at the wall. I continued.

"But you know nothing, and you tell me Mrs Fabersham does not have anything to do with this, even though there is nothing to it."

"You wouldn't know anything about the documents if I hadn't told you about them." Bakerson said.

I got up and walked to the door.

"The steward will see to your needs. If you have a further statement to make, then ask them to call for me."

"You're not leaving me 'ere to rot are you?" Bakerson said.

He jumped to his feet and strode to the door. The steward was the same height as Bakerson but broader at the shoulders. He stepped in front of Bakerson, stopping him.

"You are right." I said. "Legally I cannot confine you to your quarters. However this airship is an international vessel and the captain has the authority to confine you."

I stepped outside and watched the steward secure the door. He assured me that he would stand guard at the door until morning.

I returned to the sitting room. I borrowed a wind-breaker from a clothes peg to protect my clothes from the rain. The double doors to the promenade deck were difficult to open as they were buffeted by the wind. I stepped out into the open deck, struggling against the rain. My shoes were instantly soaked.

The killer must have stood here, by the window, for several long moments aiming his revolver. I pointed my hand at the bullet hole, pretending that I held a gun. The killer must have been an exceptional shot to be able to shoot her at this range in the wind and rain.

The wind moaned and screamed, caught in this small windswept valley between the balloon and the promenade deck. I drew the wind-breaker tighter and shivered. Thunder rumbled in the distance and I waited in vain for the next lightening flash. The storm still raged but less fiercely. There was a rhythm to the downpour as it marched across the promenade decks in sheets of icy chill.

I stood staring through the rain splashed window. The sitting room was brightly lit. Each figure inside stood out in stark relief compared to the darkness of the storm outside.

"What if I'm wrong?" I said out loud. The wind caught my words and ripped them away. "What if Mrs Fabersham was not the target but instead Mrs Colchester or Mrs Potts were the targets? Bakerson and Lord and Lady Vellance sat beyond them, could the killer have been aiming at them?"

I re-entered the airship cabin through the side door, the one the killer must have used. I stood in the quietness of the hall removing the wind-breaker. A puddle of water dripped on the floor. I removed my shoes, returned to my room and placed them on the steam pipes to dry.

It was unlikely that Bakerson or the Vellances were the target. It would have been easier for the killer to have simply moved to a different window rather than shoot through a gossip of ladies.

I resolved to move faster. In my eyes, it was likely that the murder of Mrs Fabersham was an accident, that the real target might be someone else. I had to confirm who the target was before they killed again.

Chapter Twenty-Three

"So who do you think it was?"

I had returned to the sitting room wearing my bedroom slippers. Elisabeth had immediately demanded that I sit with her and my cousin Imogen.

"Who is what dear?" I asked.

"The killer of course." Elisabeth said. "We have to find him before tomorrow when we return to London."

"I had quite forgotten about that." I remarked dryly.

Elisabeth gave me a look that I normally only received from my cousin Imogen.

The steward saved me from further questions by bringing a pot of tea.

"What I need to do is to confirm where everyone was at the time of the murder, find out who had an alibi and who did not. That will help us reduce the list of suspects."

"Does that mean that Mr Bakerson is innocent?" Imogen asked.

"Possibly." I said. "I do not want to dismiss him as he could have been working with an accomplice."

I did not add that spite probably played a part as well. Mr Bakerson was a bad sort. Although I could not prove him guilty, I was sure he was complicit in something illegal. The documents were likely stolen, perhaps I could arrest him handling stolen goods, or even for treason?

I was not proud of myself but, after twenty years of experience in the constabulary, arrests were very important to me.

Elisabeth changed seats to one with a writing table. She stacked her pink sheets to the side and started a clean sheet. She cleaned the nib of her fountain pen.

I dictated to her the events of the murder, the time, and the actions I undertook.

"Mr Bakerson definitely is innocent of killing Mrs Fabersham however he may have an accomplice or otherwise be complicit in the crime. Lord and Lady Vellance similarly are innocent."

I paused for a moment in thought before continuing.

"However Lord Vellance did leave the sitting room shortly after the lights went out." I hesitated again. "I do not think that he had the time to hurry outside in the dark but it may have been possible. Mrs Potts, Mrs Colchester, Miss Elisabeth Murphy, and Lady Imogen LaRue were also present when the lights went out."

After tea I asked for the steward who had been on duty during the power-cut. He appeared a few minutes later. It was Rodney 'Rodders' Jones.

"Take a seat Mr Jones." I said.

I indicated the free seat in front of me. Rodders sat on the edge of his seat, clearly nervous to be interviewed by me again.

"You were in the corridor of the bedroom wing this evening when the lights went out?" I asked.

"Yes sir. I came on duty just after dinner. I cover the dinner to breakfast shift. The corridor does not have any natural light as you know sir so, when the main electrical lights went out, it is absolutely pitch dark."

"Was anyone in the corridor with you?"

"Not when the lights went out. But there were plenty of 'to-ing and fro-ing' of people walking back and forth in the dark. People screaming and tripping. It was scary."

"Can you identify anyone that was there?"

"Well I 'eard Mrs Charles talking loudly to her 'usband in her room. So they were there. The German, Mr 'eiss, opened the door to the corridor. 'e 'ad the clockwork light turned on so I could see 'im and 'is wife clearly. They kindly lent me their light so I could go into the smoking room and collect the spare clockwork lights from there. Lord Vellance found me there collecting the lights."

"How long did it take Lord Vellance to find you?"

"I could not even guess, sir. I was in the smoking room by then so he definitely joined me there."

"And you say you did not remain in the corridor all the time? Did you see Mr Ashton during that period?"

"Mr Ashton was in his room. He did not realise that the main electrical lights had failed. He was trying to read a book using the pale clockwork light in his room and only realised there was something wrong when he heard the screams later."

"Thank you for that." I said.

I started to dismiss the steward, then called him back.

"One last question. You said you heard Mrs Charles, but did you see her? Did you see or hear Mr Charles?"

"I didn't see either of them." He paused for a moment in thought. "Their door was closed so they would have been using clockwork lights. They probably didn't know that the main lights went out either. I don't rightly remember sir if I 'eard Mr Charles. He obviously must 'ave been there though."

"Obviously." I said and dismissed him.

"But that is everyone accounted for." Elisabeth said. "They all have an alibi."

She quickly pored through her notes and counted up each of the passengers. I lifted my hand to forestall her next comment.

"Yes, they all have an alibi." I said. "We need to see who has a valid alibi and who is lying."

Elisabeth passed me her sheets of pink paper. I spread them out on the table.

"As an example." I said. "Lord Vellance went to fetch a steward to provide us with some lights. He left the sitting room almost as soon as the main electrical lights went out, but the steward confirmed that Lord Vellance took a long time to get there. Did he have enough time to step out of the side door to the promenade deck, shoot Mrs Fabersham and return to the smoking room?"

"The rain was very heavy at that time." Elisabeth pointed out. "He would have been soaked to the skin."

"No. There is a peg next to the door with wind-breakers. He could have borrowed one before he stepped out to the deck."

"So do you think he did it?"

"Perhaps." I said. I shrugged, unwilling to commit myself. "Roland Ashton is just as good a candidate."

"But the steward said he was in his room."

"He could have sneaked from his room in the dark, murdered Mrs Fabersham, and returned to his room before anyone was any the wiser. Then there is Simon Charles."

"He was in his room with his wife."

"Perhaps, or perhaps Mrs Charles talked loudly to pretend that her husband was still with her." I said. "If he was in the room with her, why was she speaking so loudly that the steward in the corridor could hear her?"

"Then he could have sneaked out in the dark while she continued talking." Elisabeth said. "I think it is him. I never trusted lawyers."

"I think if he killed Mr Herts, he would have found it easier to do it through the use of a lawsuit." I said.

Elisabeth laughed. I was startled. The mood in the airship was morose because of the callous deaths. In mutual respect to Mrs Fabersham, or perhaps a fear that the seat was cursed, meant that the seat, previously occupied by Mrs Fabersham when she died, was empty.

I surveyed the sitting room.

Mrs Colchester, Lady Vellance and Imogen had taken seats in the centre of the lounge. They were talking loudly about knitting or crochet or some such. Perhaps too loudly. I suspected that Lady Vellance was on the edge of hysteria and the ladies were using the comfort of a familiar task to calm her. Mrs Potts, I was informed, had been sedated and was being treated privately in her room by the doctor.

The men had moved to the smoking area, I resolved to make my way there. I had some further questions to put to Mr Ashton. I thanked Elisabeth for her help. Naturally, as a woman, she could not join me in the smoking lounge. Naturally, she was annoyed about this and returned to Imogen in a huff.

She reluctantly gave me her notes regarding the interview with Roland Ashton. I borrowed her fountain pen. I got up to leave when Kurt Heiss entered the sitting room. His normally pale face was flushed, his lips curled. He strode across the room and stopped in front of me.

"I demand that you explain yourself at once."

Chapter Twenty-Four

"I have been informed that you are about to arrest me, Detective Sergeant."

I winced at his cold tone of voice. I invited him to sit at the table and Elisabeth joined us. She chose a fresh sheet of pink writing paper and waited with her fountain pen poised. I tried in vain to catch her eye.

"Who has informed you of that Mr Heiss?" I asked.

"Does it matter who informed me?" He said. He made no effort to hide his German accent. "I am a diplomat and, under the terms of the Wiener Kongress, the Congress of Vienna, I have the right to know if I am to be arrested. Further, I have the right to contact my embassy to inform them of any detention which will result in my not being able to carry out my duties."

"I am fully aware of your diplomatic rights." I lied. "I do not have any intention of arresting you, nor of charging you with any crime. However my job is to get to the truth."

"The truth? You would never succeed as a politician."

"Politicians in parliament are like a special breed of flower." I said. "I keep them as far from me as possible. They may look pretty from a distance, but they are often useless and expensive."

Mr Heiss snorted. He leaned back and crossed one elegant leg over another as he lit a cigar. Dorothy Heiss entered. I stood as she approached and waited for her to sit. She smiled reassuringly to her husband.

"I do have another few questions for you as a matter of fact." I said. "The murder of Mrs Fabersham occurred earlier when the main electrical lights failed. The steward mentioned that he spoke to you briefly?"

"That is correct." Dorothy Heiss said. "Our suite is lit by the clockwork lights. We did not realise that there was problems with the main electrical lights until we heard the disturbance outside."

"What was the disturbance?"

"The steward had fallen over in the dark and was calling for assistance. We had two clockwork lights, one for our sitting room and the other for the bedroom, so we gave him the light for the bedroom. He gratefully took the light and said he was going to the smoking lounge to get more."

"You returned to your room at that time?"

"The corridor was dark so, yes we returned to our room."

"So you do have a partial alibi for the period when Mrs Fabersham was murdered."

"Partial alibi?" Dorothy Heiss lifted a carefully manicured eyebrow.

"You say that you returned to your room but either of you could have just as easily sneaked out in the dark and shot her from the promenade deck outside the sitting room."

I kept a pleasant tone of voice when I made the accusation. Dorothy Heiss's response was unexpected. She laughed.

"So you believe that we killed her and your proof is that we stayed in our room when it was chaotic and dark?" Dorothy Heiss said.

"When you put it that way, it does sound silly." I said. "You have both spent a lot of time in your suite instead of socialising with other passengers."

"I found the other passengers obnoxious." Mr Heiss said. "Are you aware that Simon Charles has created a betting ring? I am the favourite to be arrested for murder. It is difficult to have a pleasant conversation with someone who is betting that we are guilty of this heinous crime and are about to be arrested."

I winced at this. I believed Simon Charles was a racist from his comments, but I could not say that out loud.

"Perhaps a different question then." I said. "We believe that the reason Mr Herts was killed was because of several documents that had come into his possession. Mr Herts had received what we believe are stolen plans for the new British Dreadnought ship. This is the most advanced steam battleship in the world." I paused for a moment. "I can imagine these plans would be very valuable, especially to the German empire. Would you agree Mr Heiss?"

"I have never heard of these plans." Mr Heiss said. "I imagine that they would be very valuable to the right buyer. Not just in Germany but in every country of the world."

I was not convinced that he did not know about the sale of the plans. As he had previously said, his job was to obtain information for his country. The plans for the Dreadnought would be the ultimate 'jewel in the crown'.

Could he have murdered Mr Herts and Mrs Fabersham for them?

Chapter Twenty-Five

I left Kurt and Dorothy Heiss talking to Elisabeth and went in search of Roland Ashton.

I was faintly disturbed. I had instinctively dismissed him and his wife from the murder of Mr Herts but I could not help feeling that he had something to do with the stolen documents. They were very valuable to his country and it would be his patriotic duty to secure them. I just hoped that this did not include murder.

Roland Ashton was enjoying a glass of whiskey with Simon Charles when I entered the smoking room. Simon Charles immediately offered me a cigar, which I accepted, and invited me to sit down.

"I thought that, with Bakerson locked up, you would be celebrating another successful case solved." Roland Ashton said. "Why are you harassing me?"

"It is not yet resolved." I said. "Although Mr Bakerson is a suspect for the murder of Mr Herts, he is innocent of the death of Mrs Fabersham. We are looking for his accomplice."

"I am astonished that you have not locked up Mr Heiss as well." Simon Charles said. "I am sure that he is complicit in the murder. Perhaps he is the paymaster, and he paid Bakerson to commit the murder."

"I have no proof of that Mr Charles."

I tried to keep a pleasant tone when I spoke, but Simon Charles somehow brought out the worst in me. His dour smile, his funeral suit, and his racist sentiment together made me uncomfortable in his presence.

"Perhaps I can speak to Mr Ashton alone." I continued. My smile was frozen on my face when I said it.

Simon Charles blinked then stood. He mumbled under his breath about the incompetence of the police constabulary which I pretended not to hear. Then left to join Lord Vellance.

"I am sorry about that." I said to Roland. "I wanted to go over the statement you had given me earlier. I thought it would be less embarrassing for me if you filled in the gaps in private."

Roland Ashton laughed out loud for a moment.

"I would not want you to feel embarrassed on my account."

I watched him relax. I wanted him to relax so I could see his reaction when I confronted him about his lies. I flipped through the pink pages of notes in Elisabeth's careful handwriting looking for a specific paragraph.

"Ahh yes. We did have a difficult interview earlier. I had a few minor details that I felt I needed to confirm."

I paused for a moment, watching him through lowered eyelashes. He was starting to nervously pull at a thread on his jacket.

"How well do you know Mr Bakerson?" I asked.

"Not very well. I have met him a few times. We are members of the same club in London. He has enjoyed hunting in the past and I did mention inviting him for a hunt."

"So you have a slight acquaintance with him or perhaps a friendship?"

"Merely an acquaintance."

"Did you know that he was going to be on this airship? Did you arrange to meet him here?"

"No, I did not."

"He made the comment that whatever you said about him is not true. Do you know what he means by that?"

"I have heard that he's a criminal. Anything that you want he can get from his 'auction'."

"So you admit to consorting with criminals?"

"What do you mean consorting?"

"Hanging around, habitually associating with the criminal class." I said.

"I never said any such thing."

"That is good." I raised my hand to stop Roland Ashton from rising. His face was flushed and he was breathing heavy. I flipped through some more notes.

"The electric lights failed earlier. Where were you?"

"I was in my room reading a book. The clockwork lights casts a poor light but just sufficient for reading."

"What was the book?"

"It was nothing, just a silly adventure story. Does it matter?" I raised an enquiring eyebrow so he continued with a heavy sigh. "It was by Jules Verne. One of the Incredible Voyages books."

I made a note on the pink sheets. Elisabeth's fountain pen wrote remarkably smoothly. I created tiny crisp letters on the sheets.

"You mentioned that you did not know and had never met Mr Herts. However Mr Bakerson said something different. He said that when he first met you, you were trying to worm your way into Mr Herts's operations. Perhaps you can enlighten me."

"There is nothing really to enlighten you about. Mr Bakerson is obviously guilty of killing Mr Herts and is trying to spread the blame."

"So you have never tried to gain Mr Herts's trust?" I asked. "Never tried to get your foot in the door? Mr Bakerson said that you are always trying to snoop around."

"He is lying."

"You knew Mr Bakerson. Mr Bakerson is an associate of Mr Herts. Mr Herts's business interests lie in Africa. You have repeatedly stated that you are an expert in Africa. Yet you insist that you have not met Mr Herts? Not tried to persuade him to make use of your knowledge?"

"Well maybe I have bumped into him once or twice." Roland Ashton said. "It is difficult not to, in a city as small as London."

The main electric lights flickered once, then came on strong. There was a cheer from the other passengers.

"Did you discuss offering him your hunting services on that once or twice occasion?" I asked.

"I always talk about hunting, whether it's my latest trophy or my next hunting trip."

"Did you offer to smuggle for him?"

"I say. These questions are getting quite outrageous."

"It is a simple question." I said. "Did you offer to smuggle for him?"

"No, I did not. Nor do I think these questions are relevant to the murder of Mr Herts or Mrs Fabersham."

"I am the person who decides what is relevant or not." I said. "We believe the murder was because of some stolen documents that were in his possession. Were you aware that Mr Herts had those documents?"

Roland Ashton refused to meet my gaze. He was studying his glass of whiskey. He threw the drink back before he answered.

"I was not aware of any such documents."

"Stop lying to me."

His body tensed. For a moment I thought he was about to throw himself at me. The moment passed.

He looked away and took a deep breath. He then leaned forward and spoke to me in a confidential whisper.

"If I tell you something, can you keep it a secret?"

"If it is relevant to the investigation, I may not be able to." I replied. "I can certainly ask that it is kept confidential if it is not of interest."

"It is, and it isn't." Roland Ashton said. He looked down at his hands then back up to meet my eyes. "I am very aware of the documents that Bakerson gave to Herts. I have been trying to ingratiate myself into Reginald Herts's community for several months in order to get close. I do not think that he trusted me, and kept me at arm's length."

"So you joined the airship to stay near him?"

"Yes, I knew that either he or Bakerson would have the documents. There is an auction in Rome in the next few days to sell the stolen documents. My job was to find out where the auction was to be held and to identify the buyers."

"You are saying it is your job." I paused for a moment. "What is your real job?"

"I work for the Secret Intelligence Bureau under Major Vernon Kell." Roland Ashton whispered. "I have been tasked with finding and recovering the plans for the new Dreadnoughts and to identify which foreign agents are interested in them."

I sat back in my chair dumbfounded. It was entirely possible that Roland Ashton was lying to me. But if he was not, I would be in trouble if I disclosed his identity. It did explain his lies earlier.

"Can you prove this?" I asked.

"Of course I cannot bloody prove it. I cannot carry identification with me in case I am ever caught."

"Then why should I believe you?"

"If you contact Major Kell, he will vouch for me."

I nodded. I had hoped that Roland Ashton was the killer but his earlier evasiveness and lies now made sense. I called a steward over and wrote a radio telegram, in the pink writing paper, addressed to Major Kell detailing that I was involved in a murder investigation and would he vouch for Roland Ashton.

"Do you know where the documents are?"

"No. Either Bakerson has them or he has hidden them somewhere. Have you checked Mrs Fabersham's room, she was quite close to Bakerson. Perhaps he gave them to her for safekeeping."

I had a sudden insight. I had checked her room but, if the killer had murdered her for the documents, perhaps she had them with her when she died. I had not checked her pocketbook.

"Does this mean you believe that I am innocent?" Roland Ashton asked.

"No, but it does mean that I am less inclined to think you are guilty." I said.

I pondered this as I excused myself and returned to the sitting room. Two murders had been committed and my main suspect had confessed to being a government spy. If this was true, I was even further from solving the murder than I thought.

Chapter Twenty-Six

The steward returned a few moments later as I sat with Imogen and Elisabeth. The radio telegram had been sent but, due to the late hour, I should not expect to receive a reply until morning. I nodded thanks and asked him if the captain would mind if I examined the dead bodies again.

"What have you found out?" Elisabeth asked.

"Nothing much except that Roland likes to read the novels by Jules Verne." I said. I related to her our discussion. I omitted the fact that Roland was part of the government's secret service. "He mentioned that he works for the government in some capacity. I have sent a radio telegram to London to confirm."

"So what are you going to do next?" Elisabeth asked.

"I am still trying to understand the reason why Mrs Fabersham was killed." I said. "If she had the documents then the killer would have searched the room for them. Why kill her? Then I realised that we have not actually searched her pockets for the documents. I may need some help from you, but only if you are willing."

Elisabeth paled slightly.

"Of course I can help."

"She most certainly cannot." Imogen said.

"She has already seen the dead body." I said. "In fact, nurses help doctors with dead patients all the time."

"I can do this, Aunt Imogen. I am not afraid." Elisabeth said.

Imogen shook her head disapprovingly but did not make a further objection.

The captain sent word that we were to be given access to the balloon again in order to look at the bodies. Elisabeth and I followed the steward up a set of different steps, this time from the kitchen. This led to a pantry in the balloon.

"This pantry is colder than the rest of the balloon." I said.

"Yes, sir." The steward replied. "The steam engine heats the rest of the balloon to help it to lift but they deliberately sectioned this part off to keep the food cool."

"It doesn't smell either." I said.

"That's right sir. The rest of the balloon has the small sacs of helium. The sacs are made from oxen entrails, which is where the smell comes from. Here in this pantry we don't have any sacs of helium, so it's just clean honest fresh air."

"This is where you keep the dead bodies?" Elisabeth asked.

"Where better, Miss. We keep them away from the rest of the food obviously but it's perfectly cold here and no one will disturb them."

The steward led us to a corner of the room where two bodies lay in repose. Each was wrapped in waterproof covering. I opened one and discovered the body of Mr Herts. He looked so peaceful. His face was relaxed in death. Just the thin slit of blood on his shirt confirmed the stab wound. I rewrapped the body.

I unwrapped the covering over Mrs Fabersham's body. The blood stuck to the covering which made it difficult to unwrap.

I heard a gulp beside me and Elisabeth gripped my arm. Her fingers were very white where she had grabbed me.

"I'm sorry." Elisabeth's face was very pale. "I was not expecting so much blood. Mr Herts's body had so little and I was expecting it to be like that."

I quietly kicked myself. I should have thought how she might react when she saw the blood.

"Perhaps I was wrong in asking you to help." I said. I gently started to lead her away.

"No, I can do this." Elisabeth said.

She knelt on the floor and, carefully avoiding all the blood, started to search through the body. She passed me Mrs Fabersham's purse along with two small books that were in her pockets.

"She does not have any documents." Elisabeth said as I helped her to her feet. "What do you have there?"

"The purse has her ticket as well as some small change." I said. "The books though are more interesting. The first one is a fiction book but, as you can see, some of the words are underlined. I wonder if this is some sort of a code."

Elisabeth stood on her tiptoes to look over my shoulder. I led her away from the body, the metallic smell of the blood was making me nauseous. I handed her the first book to look at and opened the second book. It was a dictionary.

"It is not a code." Elisabeth said. "Look, only the bigger words are underlined. She was trying to teach herself to read, poor thing."

I shook my head. The murder of an innocent young lady was always difficult on your feeling. Each time you experienced the sadness of a life lost anew.

Elisabeth returned to Mrs Fabersham's body and gently started to rewrap the waterproof sheeting over the corpse.

"This was to be her honeymoon with her husband. She only married him recently and now she is just a bloody footnote in a newspaper's column. Unlike Herts, barely a drop of blood on him and I bet he takes up a full page spread in the gazette."

I froze.

There was an elusive thought in the back of my mind about Mr Herts's body. I tried to track it down but it evaded me. It was important though. Something of what she said was important.

"Shall we return downstairs?" Elisabeth said.

She cocked her head looking at me curiously. I waved my hand for her to be silent.

I closed my eyes, concentrating. It wasn't the comment about the newspaper. It was the body, something about the body. Something about how bloody Mrs Fabersham's body was. My eyes snapped open.

"The bodies."

I walked over to Mrs Fabersham's body and pulled back the wrapping. The hole in the centre of her chest was messy. Her whole dress had soaked in blood and the waterproof wrapping was messy from where the blood had spread.

I crossed to Mr Herts's body and spread out the waterproof wrapping. There was a tiny red slit in his shirt where the scissors had stabbed him. His eyes were closed and he lay in repose.

"Compare these two bodies." I said. "Both died by chest trauma. What is the difference between the two?"

Elisabeth looked at me in confusion.

"One is bloodier than the other." Elisabeth said. "But Mrs Fabersham was shot, surely that would be bloodier?"

"It would be. But you would still expect Herts to have bled some more than this. Also look at Mr Herts's eyes. They are closed. It is almost as if he was asleep. Don't you think?"

I was getting excited and my accent always gets stronger when I'm excited.

"Well I suppose, yes."

"It explains it all. It explains why there was no outcry, it explains why he is wearing shoes late at night. It explains why his waistcoat is done up wrong. In fact look, see his shoes, they are tied wrong as well. I mean it explains everything."

"What's wrong with how his shoes are tied?" Elisabeth asked.

"Yes, well, they are tied correctly from our perspective. The left lace is over the right lace. Mr Herts was right handed. From his perspective the right lace is over the left lace."

"Perhaps that is how he ties his laces. Perhaps he is left handed."

"No. He is right handed. Look his pocket watch is in the right hand side of his waistcoat." I emptied his pockets. "His keys and spare change are in his right coat pocket. His handkerchief is in his right trouser pocket. He is right handed."

"But what does that mean?" Elisabeth said.

I could not understand why she didn't understand.

"It's obvious isn't it?" I said.

Elisabeth still did not react.

"It's obvious because it means he did not tie the laces himself. Someone else put his shoes on for him. The waistcoat was done up wrong because someone else put it on him."

Elisabeth shrugged, she was still confused.

"Let us put the facts together." I said, trying hard not to sound impatient. "He was dressed by someone else. Why could he not dress himself? We have also got a stab wound in the centre of his chest. Why is not bloody? Perhaps not as bloody as the bullet wound that the poor Mrs Fabersham received but you would expect some blood. Lastly, why are his eyes closed?"

I hesitated for a moment. Elisabeth shrugged again.

"The reason was, he was already dead." I said. "This is probably what happened. Last night he played whist until very late. At some point someone must have given him a poison. Perhaps slipped into his drink."

"The stomach ache." Elisabeth said. "The doctor thought that his nausea was due to air sickness. Was that the poison?"

"I think so." I said. "The doctor did not examine him or ask about symptoms. I remember someone saying that Herts was sharp with the doctor who gave him one of his airsickness tablets?"

Elisabeth spent a few moments flicking through her notes.

"Doctor Peters said that Mr Herts had an upset stomach and wanted a sedative to help him sleep."

I nodded.

"Even better. He drank the sedative, with a whiskey chaser if I remember correctly, and went to bed. The poison killed him in his sleep. The murderer entered the cabin much later, when the steward was distracted, and searched the cabin for the documents. He dressed the body and stabbed it with scissors."

"That would be the mysterious figure. Why did he do that?"

"Because he did not want anyone to remember that he spent the evening in Mr Herts's company. He did not want people to think Mr

Herts was poisoned. He wanted people to think that Mr Herts was murdered by the scissors."

"And the pipe?"

"A distraction. The murderer stole both the pipe and the scissors earlier in the evening. The pipe was to cast the blame on Mr Heiss and the scissors was to cast the blame on Mrs Colchester."

"So Mr Heiss and Mrs Colchester are innocent?"

I thought for a moment. Although I was now convinced of Mr Heiss's innocence, I did not want to exclude him from my enquiries.

"No. Let us include him as a suspect for now."

I looked down at Mr Herts. The more I found out about him, the more I was convinced that society was better off without him.

"You are convinced this is how the murder happened. All this is based on how he tied his shoes and the lack of blood?"

"It is the only thing that makes sense." I said.

I rewrapped the two bodies securely with the waterproof blankets, thanked the steward, and descended to the kitchen again.

"What are our next steps?" Elisabeth asked.

"The same as always. Find the murderer before he kills again."

Chapter Twenty-Seven

It was almost dinner time so I retired to my room briefly to change for dinner. I would never dress so formally for dinner at home but, because we were on a cruise, Imogen had insisted that I bring a dinner jacket. I quickly washed and changed.

The ladies would take longer to dress so I stole a few moments to read my book. Dr Watson was describing the intolerable conditions in the Indian subcontinent when I heard a quiet knock on my door.

I placed my book on the chair and opened the door. Kurt Heiss was standing at the door with his hand raised for a second knock. He was already dressed for dinner.

"Is this an inopportune moment?" Kurt Heiss asked. His German accent was quite strong.

I invited him into my small room. Luckily the maid had made my bed earlier and straightened my belongings so the room looked reasonably acceptable for visitors. I offered him the chair and sat on the bed.

Kurt lifted the book I had been reading and smiled at the title.

"The Biography of Dr John H. Watson, A Journey of Remembrances." He murmured. "I enjoyed his first book, the Reminiscences of John H Watson. He has a delightful literary style."

"He is very humble." I said. "He places his success at the feet of his colleagues and refuses to take any credit. I think I would like him." I paused for a moment, Kurt Heiss was looking uncomfortable. "What can I do for you Kurt?"

"I came to apologise for my ill-mannered comments earlier." Kurt Heiss said. He shrugged. "You have been very fair to me and I was unduly angry. The comments from certain fellow passengers against

Germany left me ill-at-ease and fearing for my safety. I do hope that you will find it in your heart to forgive me."

I smiled and stood, offering my hand for him to shake.

There is a certain bond between men that grows over time. It becomes friendship and trust then grows into love. It almost always starts with a handshake. I shook his hand knowing in my heart that this was the kind of man whom I could depend on and trust.

There was a knock on the door which interrupted further conversation. Elisabeth's voice followed the knock to confirm that she and Imogen were waiting for me. I apologised to Kurt and dragged out my valise to put away my book.

That was when I realised that something was wrong.

My valise was empty. My faithful revolver was missing. It had been stolen.

I cursed with a fluency that would have turned Imogen pale and searched the bottom of the wardrobe in vain.

"What is wrong?" Kurt asked.

"My revolver is missing." I said through gritted teeth. "I suspect that the murderer used it to kill Mrs Fabersham."

I stood up and stormed across the room to the door. I flung the door open to Elisabeth's startled face.

"Steward." I shouted.

The man jerked off his chair and half ran towards me. I could feel my nostrils' flaring. My chest was tight was suppressed rage. I wanted to grab him by the collar and shake him.

"Who has been in my room today?" I demanded.

"No one." The steward squeaked.

"Find out from the day steward if there has been anyone near my room."

Kurt put his hand on my arm and restrained me.

"What?" I demanded.

"You will not help anyone by losing your temper." Kurt said.

"What has happened?" Imogen asked.

"Someone has stolen my revolver." I said.

The steward came running back, a second steward in tow. I recognised the steward from seeing him at his post earlier. He was not wearing a tie and his jacket was undone.

"Have you been at your post all day?" I asked.

"Yes, sir. But I have been up and down to the kitchen, helping passengers, so I have not been actually sitting on my seat all day."

"Did you see anyone in my room?"

"Just the maid, sir. She did all the beds while everyone was at breakfast this morning. Is there something the matter, sir?"

"Nothing is the matter." I said through gritted teeth. "Nothing at all."

I dismissed the steward. He gave me a puzzled look, then left.

"No one sees anything." I said.

Imogen placed her hand on my shoulder and waited until I calmed down.

"Who knew that you had brought your revolver on holiday with you?" Elisabeth asked.

"Everyone." I said. "If you remember, I dropped my valise as I climbed the gangplank. The revolver bounced free and slid to the ground."

"It is not your fault." Imogen said. "Let us return to the dining room. Dinner will be served in the next few minutes and you will feel better after you have something to eat."

I nodded and let her lead me to the dining room. Kurt excused himself and rejoined his wife. I sat numbly at the table, thoughts whirling through my head. Chief among them was the thought that I was responsible for April Fabersham's death. It was my revolver that killed her. If I had not brought it on-board she would likely be still alive.

"Soup?"

The steward was waiting patiently at my side. By his expression he had asked the question before and I had not heard. I nodded to him and he doled me a bowlful.

Cousin Imogen was right. My body decided it was hungry when it smelled the food. Before I knew it, the bowl was empty and the second course was laid on the table. By the third course I had decided what I need to do.

"We need to go through the notes you made." I told Elisabeth. "Examine everything we have seen and heard. The answers to these clues must be there somewhere. Who killed Mr Herts? Who stole the plans? Who killed Mrs Fabersham?"

"You're saying that you do not think that the plans were stolen by the killer?" Elisabeth asked.

"I am saying that I do not want to make that assumption. The killer may have stolen the plans or Mr Herts may have given the plans to someone, or someone else may have stolen them."

"Or he could have hidden them." Imogen said.

"Or he could have hidden them of course." I said.

I blinked.

I jumped to my feet, knocking the wine glass over in my excitement and hurried from the dining room. I ran down the steps to the bedroom wing. The steward was sitting on his chair.

"Come with me." I snapped.

I strode to the end suite belonging to Mr Herts and waited impatiently for the steward to unlock the door. Imogen had given me the answer. Mr Herts did not trust anyone in his business. For a prize as valuable as these plans, he would not have left them sitting in a valise where a maid would find it or someone could steal it. Nor would he entrust the plans to an accomplice. He had hidden it in his room and I had a good guess where.

The door had finally opened and I stepped into the room stopping at the door. The room was in chaos. Someone had entered the suite and torn everything apart, searching for the plans.

The valise and the trunk had been opened, their contents discarded on the floor. A slit in the lining of each showed that it had been searched. In the bedroom, I could see the mattress was slit open and the cotton filling torn out and strewn around.

"At a guess, you did not see anyone enter this suite either." I said dryly to the steward.

I smiled at the chaos. There was one place in the room that had not been searched. The smoke extractor fan. When I had first examined the room I had wound up the mechanism and tested it, and then ignored it as it appeared to be broken.

I crossed the room to the extractor fan.

"What are you doing sir?" The steward's voice was respectful but a little confused.

"I am trying to work out why this extractor fan does not work." I said.

I reached up to the mechanism and wound it slightly before turning it on. There was a whirring noise but I could not feel the air moving.

"Help me open this please." I said.

I felt around the underside of the mechanism until I felt a catch, unlocked the catch and the front of the extractor fan fell free. The cogs of the clockwork mechanism were revealed inside. A small parcel of paper fell to the floor with a thump. I picked it up. The sheaf of paper was tied up with a knotted string. I was able to tease a corner free without undoing the knot and flicked through complicated diagrams of the deck plans of a ship.

"Eureka." I said turning to the steward. "Eureka indeed."

I returned to my bedroom for a few minutes and, using a small knife I borrowed from the steward, sliced open my book. The Biography of John H Watson. A few moments after that I was able to return in triumph to the dining room carrying the parcel of paper. The parcel was secured very tightly again by the string.

"What is the matter?" Imogen asked. "Everyone was looking at you when you sprinted out of the room."

I dropped the parcel on the table with a thump.

"What is that?" Elisabeth asked. "Are those the plans? Where did you find them?"

"I found where Mr Herts had hidden them." I said in a clear voice. I could see the other passengers in the dining room look up in interest. "The killer had searched his compartment but did not search the clockwork extraction fan. The documents were hidden in there."

"Are they actual plans of the dreadnought?" Kurt Heiss asked, his eyes alight with interest.

"They are certainly plans of a ship." I said. "As you can see I have not examined them further. I am not qualified to look at them further. For that matter, I suspect it would be illegal for me to examine them."

"What are you going to do with them then?" Simon Charles asked.

"We will be returning to London in the morning." I said. "I will keep them in my possession until then."

"You are very brave to do that." Edith Charles said, flashing me a dazzling smile. "The murderer will undoubtedly be looking for those plans."

"Very brave, or perhaps very stupid." I said. I returned her smile. "We will see which by morning."

Chapter Twenty-Eight

"You have found the plans but we have still not found the murderer." Elisabeth said.

We had retired to our usual table in the sitting room. The package was in the middle of the table. I had my back to the door, facing towards the windows. It was quite dark outside and the windows reflected the light back into the room. It was an imperfect mirror but meant I could watch for shadows from outside as well as watch my fellow passengers inside.

Imogen joined Mrs Potts and Mrs Colchester at the window.

"Let us take the necessary time to read through the interviews we have conducted and see if we have missed anything." I said.

With the occasional glance at the window, we bent to our task. We spent a pleasant hour reading through the individual interviews, sometimes commenting on the notes.

"The four that were playing whist last night were: Reginald Herts; Simon Charles; Kurt Heiss; and Lord Horace Vellance." Elisabeth said. "Do you think one of them could be the murderer?"

A steward had entered the sitting room and was standing unsure if he could approach. I sat up straight, stretched my back, and waved him forward.

"A radio telegram for you, sir."

I took the proffered note and quickly read it.

"No reply." I said to the steward and dismissed him.

Elisabeth's eyes were alive with curiosity.

"Radio telegram message from London regarding Roland Ashton." I said.

"Well?"

"In answer to your question, yes." I said. "Heiss and Vellance both have a motive for killing him."

"I meant about the radio telegram." Elisabeth said.

I passed the message over. Elisabeth read it aloud.

"ROLAND ASHTON ONE OF MINE STOP GIVE HIM EVERY ASSISTANCE STOP K"

"What does that mean?" Elisabeth asked.

"It means that Roland Ashton is either innocent or playing a very deep game." I replied. "We will need to look elsewhere for the murderer."

"Mr Heiss seemed very eager when you mentioned that you had found the plans."

"I would have been surprised if he wasn't. Germany would be eager to get their hands on those plans. That still does not mean that he committed the murder."

"You have dismissed him as the murderer. You did not seem to think that Lord Vellance was the killer either. That leaves only Mr Charles, do you think he is the killer?"

"I have not dismissed Lord Vellance." I said. "He did leave the sitting room after the lights went out so he had time to run around to the sitting room windows and shoot. As for Mr Charles." I hesitated for a moment, picking my words with care. "He does not have a motive, that I know of, to kill Mr Herts. Yet I do not trust him."

"What do you trust then?"

"I trust my instincts," I gestured at the pink pages, "and I trust these notes."

Elisabeth sighed and started reading again.

"This is interesting." Elisabeth said a few moments later.

I raised an eyebrow.

"We interviewed Mrs Potts regarding the mysterious figure but we never finished the interview. If you recall, the airship broke free of the anchors."

"Well spotted." I said. "Now perhaps is a good time to conclude the interview."

I stood up and joined Mrs Potts who was sitting by the window drinking tea.

"Is it convenient to disturb you for a few moments, Mrs Potts?" I asked. "We did not get the opportunity to finish our interview."

I was mindful of her deafness and had spoken in a loud voice. I could see in the reflection from the window several heads turn and a shadow got up and left the room.

"Is now really a good time?" Imogen asked. "We have only just received a pot of tea. Give us five minutes, please."

I apologised for my short-sightedness and returned to my table.

"Mrs Potts did see something." Elisabeth said. "In the last entry of the interview she stated that she was 'very surprised at the footwear' of the mysterious figure."

"What a puzzling statement to make, I wonder what she meant by that." I said.

"Perhaps she meant that the shoes were unusually small or very large."

Something about shoes bothered me. Sometimes I feel I am the most intelligent man in the room, I can make great leaps of insight. This wasn't one of those moments. It wasn't the shoes of Mr Herts, we had already resolved that to my satisfaction. There was something else. I shrugged, dismissing it. If it was important, it would come back to me.

"Or perhaps the colour of the shoes were different, or the design." Elisabeth continued.

"Have you noticed anyone with unusually small or large feet?" I asked.

"Roland Ashton has very large feet."

I stared at her.

"It is something that women notice." Elisabeth said.

"Perhaps it is that." I said.

"Do you think that she would be able to identify who the murderer is just from his size of feet?" Elisabeth asked.

"Not conclusively." I said. "Not enough to take to court and gain a conviction, but it would mean that we could narrow our investigation to that one man."

"Does that mean that she is in danger?"

I thought for a moment.

"No, probably not. If the killer wanted to get rid of her, they would already have attempted to murder her. I'll keep an eye out for her just in case."

I stared across at the ladies. It is a weakness in my character, my impatience. I was probably going to be spending the next few hours in my cabin trying to protect the plans from a murderer who had killed twice and would not hesitate to kill a third time. As well as that, the killer had my revolver. I was unarmed. It was going to be a long night.

Elisabeth tapped the parcel of paper on the table.

"Please don't." I said. "The string is a bit loose and I do not want it all coming apart."

"All this killing. All this misery. All for just a small parcel of paper. Why do people go to all this trouble for something so petty?"

"If that was a parcel of Bank of England banknotes would you still consider it petty?" I asked.

Elisabeth shrugged, but she stopped tapping the parcel.

I glanced back at the gossip of ladies drinking tea at their table by the window. They were still talking.

I saw a vague shape outside the window.

Chapter Twenty-Nine

At that moment, I realised with a flash of insight why Mrs Fabersham was killed. She was not shot because of her relationship to Bakerson. She had been shot because she had the misfortune to sit next to Mrs Potts. The killer feared that Mrs Potts had seen more than she had revealed. That she knew enough to incriminate him.

These thoughts burned through my head as I threw myself towards the light switch. I shouted 'get down' and flicked the light switch off. The main lights went dark a moment before a revolver barked. The flash from the gun revealed the shape of the figure outside on the promenade deck.

He started to run back towards the side door. I bounded after him, or tried to as I collided with a small table. My feet entangled, I crashed to the floor. I rolled unsteadily to my feet and wrenched open the double doors to the promenade deck.

The deck was empty, the killer had escaped again.

I called for lights and a few moments later the main light was switched on. Elisabeth was standing at the door. The light switch in hand.

"Oh God. Mrs Potts."

I dropped to my knees beside her. Imogen was cradling her head very tenderly. Mrs Charles ran to the door to call the doctor. Mrs Colchester sat with her mouth open in shock.

There was a streak of red on Mrs Potts's sleeve. I closed my eyes with relief and said a silent prayer. The bullet had clipped her upper arm, she was alive.

"Get a glass of water." I said to Kurt. He nodded and trotted to the trolley where he poured a drink.

By the time the doctor arrived, the other passengers had appeared from their rooms and stood in dismay. The doctor bustled in, two stewards followed him with a stretcher. They stopped confused when they saw Mrs Potts sitting up.

"I had been informed that Mrs Potts had been killed." Doctor Peters said.

"Happily the report was inaccurate." I said.

The doctor led Mrs Potts to a quiet corner and helped her sit while he attended her arm.

"This is intolerable." Lord Vellance said. "It is outrageous that, not only is the killer still at large but, you are not taking basic precautions to protect us from the deranged killer. I demand that the ship's captain takes over the investigation and that we return to London at once for someone more competent to be put in charge."

"It is certainly within your right to appeal to the captain." I said. I signalled to a steward and requested the captain to join us. "Perhaps to relieve your anxieties I will relate to you what I have found out so far. You can decide if you wish for me to continue my investigation or to replace me."

I called for another steward and instructed them to arrange the chairs in the sitting room and to drag the podium from the smoking lounge into a prominent position. I placed my parcel of papers in the back of the podium next to the hidden chalice. The captain arrived while this was being arranged.

"The wind has died down so I have instructed the crew to cast off." Captain Harvey said. "We will reach London by about six o'clock in the morning. Until then, I am happy that Detective Sergeant Ignatius Brown remains in charge."

"Thank you." I said. "I have decided to relate the conclusions I have formed regarding this case. Can I ask that Mr Bakerson joins us also?"

The captain agreed and we waited for a few moments for Bakerson to appear. He was sullen. I sat him down between Lord Vellance and Simon Charles. The two burly stewards stood behind him.

"With the attempt on the life of Mrs Potts, does that mean that Mr Bakerson is innocent?" Elisabeth asked.

"Not necessarily, I believe the killer had an accomplice." I said.

This was sufficient to quieten the room.

"Perhaps if I can go through the steps of my investigation." I said.

I detailed how we had discovered that Mr Herts had been dressed after his murder and the lack of blood around the puncture wound. This led me to believe that he had been killed by poison earlier in the evening.

"I would be grateful if you could spare the doctor to confirm what type of poison had actually killed him." I said to the captain.

"How was the poison administered?" Kurt Heiss asked.

"I considered several methods." I said. "The most obvious was that the doctor was not wearing his spectacles yesterday evening and had accidentally given Mr Herts too large a dose of sedative or indeed accidentally poisoned Mr Herts."

The doctor jerked upright in shock. He paled. His mouth opened but he could not speak for a moment.

"That is outrageous."

"Calm yourself, doctor." I said. "Obviously I dismissed that. It would be too great a coincidence for the victim to be accidentally killed by you then murdered later by a pair of scissors. But it did get me thinking why was he killed twice."

I paused. I had everyone's rapt attention and it felt good. Perhaps in another life I could be a lecturer or a teacher.

"As to the method of poison, I have seen poison administered by a dart from a blowgun, hidden in a cigar or food, sprayed into a person's face, even heard of a murder committed by stabbing the victim in the leg with a sharp umbrella."

I smiled at the memory. It had been one of my first cases and was one of which I was most proud.

"I think however it was slipped into his drink. A slow acting poison which gave him some nausea that could be easily dismissed as airsickness. He died in his sleep."

Mrs Colchester snorted. I raised an eyebrow at her but she refused to say anything.

"For someone who lived by the sword, dying in his sleep seems to have been too good for him." I said. "However the killer was not looking for justice for the many crimes that he allegedly committed. He was looking for some documents."

I reached for the package of papers on the shelf in the pulpit and raised the parcel high before letting it drop on the book-stand part of the pulpit. It landed with an impressive thump.

"He killed Mr Herts for it. He killed Mrs Fabersham. He tried to kill Mrs Potts."

"But Mrs Potts did not have the documents, nor did Mrs Fabersham." Imogen said.

"That is correct." I said. "I believe, and hopefully can prove, that Mrs Fabersham was killed by accident. The real target was Mrs Potts."

There was some consternation among my audience at my comments. Mr Bakerson had dropped his face into his hands. His shoulders shook. One of the stewards patted his shoulder in sympathy.

"The killer had murdered Mr Herts in his sleep so that he would have access to the suite to search it for the documents. He dressed Mr Herts and then stabbed him with the scissors to try and throw me off the track. While the steward was distracted he left the room only to find that the steward had returned early. Mrs Potts was with the steward. The killer realised that Mrs Potts was likely to recognise him so later he attempted to kill Mrs Potts."

"Why did he try and kill Mrs Potts and not the steward?"

"Mrs Potts recognised the shoes of the killer. My lovely assistant Elisabeth, gave me part of the reason when she said that it was something that a woman would notice. Additionally, Mrs Potts tried to tell me in her interview. But because of the noise of the storm and her deafness we had to shout. The killer heard my question and Mrs Potts's answer."

I paused for a moment.

"The killer was in the room at the time."

Chapter Thirty

There was a moment of silence then the questions started to tumble out from the other passengers.

"You mean that you know who the killer is?"

"How can you be so sure?"

"Why didn't you tell us before?"

"Is it something that you can prove?"

I raised my hands for silence. I tried to imagine the picture that I probably displayed. I was standing behind God's pulpit with my arms raised like a priest about to pass judgement over a member of his flock. If I had worn a high collar on my shirt, that would have completed the picture.

"Please, I have a theory. Perhaps if I can relay the facts to you first, you can judge for yourself."

I waited a few more moments for the passengers to regain their seats before continuing.

"It was the only way that the killer could know that I had attached importance to the shoes. I did not manage to question Mrs Potts further at the time as I was distracted when the ship broke loose. Then Mrs Fabersham was murdered."

I paused, reflecting. It was perhaps my fault that she had died. If only I had been quicker at putting the clues together.

"The killer shot her from outside on the promenade deck. It was windy and very wet and the killer borrowed a waterproof coat to protect him from the rain. I went outside later to examine the scene. I did not find anything of interest but one thing I did notice was how quickly my shoes were soaked by the rain. I put them on the steam pipe in my room to dry. The killer's shoes were similarly soaked as well."

"You mean that the killer had wet shoes?"

"I didn't see anyone with wet shoes."

"Yes." I said. "He changed his shoes. He realised how damning the wet shoes would look so he changed into bedroom slippers."

The killer turned pale. I turned to look in his eyes.

"Didn't you, Mr Charles?"

Chapter Thirty-One

Simon Charles jumped to his feet.

"This is outrageous," he spluttered, "you cannot accuse someone of murder just because of your own incompetence. I demand to see your proof."

"It was you who put poison in Mr Herts's whiskey." I said. "It was you who sent the steward on an errand while your accomplice, your wife Edith Charles, searched the room for the documents and stabbed his corpse with the scissors."

The two stewards moved from their station behind Mr Bakerson and restrained Mr Charles.

"She was the mysterious figure who walked down the corridor. When the steward returned at the exact wrong moment, she could not slip back into your room but instead brushed past the steward and Mrs Potts. Mrs Potts recognised her shoes. Your wife slipped back into your room while the steward was distracted with Mrs Potts. Later you were in the sitting room when I was interviewing Mrs Potts. She recognised your wife's shoes. You realised the significance of her answer and resolved to kill her. Later you waited until the steward was distracted and stole my revolver."

I saw Edith Charles grimace, I was on the right track.

"You caused the blackout, I don't know how, but I suspect that you removed the thin wire from your bed and attached it to the electrical system then lowered it into the storm. A lightning strike completed it by overloading the system. During the blackout Mrs Charles talked very loudly to you, but no one heard your reply. She was supplying an alibi. You had already slipped out to the promenade deck in the dark where you tried to shoot Mrs Potts. You missed. Mrs Fabersham died."

Tears appeared in Marcus Bakerson eyes. But all eyes were focussed on Mr Charles who wrenched at the two stewards, trying to free his arms.

"Hold him carefully gentlemen." I said. "He still has my revolver."

Other passengers jumped to their feet and clustered round, staring in fascination at Simon Charles. They were careful not to get too close to him. His face went through a transformation of different expressions from fear to anger to hunted animal.

"You changed your shoes to bedroom slippers when you returned, careful not to leave any wet footprints that would have accused you. Then you realised I had not picked up on Mrs Potts's comments and you decided to lie low. It was only when I suggested to Mrs Potts to finish the interview that you slipped out with my revolver to the promenade deck again. To try to kill her again."

I paused. Simon Charles was breathing very heavily. The seams of his undertaker jacket had torn during his struggle with the stewards. Edith Charles sat on her chair, her purse on her knees, a slight smile tugged at her lips.

"Did I get anything wrong?" I asked.

Edith Charles flashed me a dazzling smile.

"Just one thing," she said, "Simon does not have your revolver. I have it."

Edith Charles produced the revolver from her purse and pointed it at the stewards holding Simon Charles.

"Let him go." Her voice had a hint of steel in it.

I waved the stewards away. Edith Charles waved the revolver at the other passengers who drew back. Mr Charles straightened his jacket. He approached me and took the parcel of paper from the podium.

"Thank you for this."

I did not reply as he rejoined his wife. They started to walk backwards towards the door.

"One question." I called.

Edith Charles pointed my revolver at me. I am not a brave man. My stomach tightened and my legs turned to jelly. The barrel looked huge. I coughed to clear my throat and tried again.

"One question. Why did you kill Mr Herts, was it just for the money?"

"We were hired to kill him." Simon Charles said. "Recovery of his papers is a bonus."

"And framing the German diplomat Mr Heiss?"

"The person who hired us demanded that." Simon Charles said.

Edith Charles elbowed him to be quiet.

"Who hired you?" I asked. "Why would he want this?"

Simon Charles turned to the door, his wife continued to point the revolver at us. He opened it and peered into the corridor.

"There is no one here." He said with surprise. "Really detective sergeant, did you really expect to be able to arrest us so easily?"

This was the moment that Marcus Bakerson became a hero.

Chapter Thirty-Two

There was a roar of fury as Marcus Bakerson pounced from his seat towards Simon Charles and grabbed him. I heard a yelp of pain from Simon Charles as something silver flashed in the light and stabbed in his stomach.

Edith Charles fired three times. Red splotches appeared in Bakerson's back as the three bullets thudded home. Bakerson slid to the floor, his face empty. A knife clattered beside him. Simon Charles was dragged to the floor as well. I could see that his stomach was bloody and ruined where he had been stabbed.

Edith Charles snatched up the parcel of papers and stood pointing the revolver at us.

"Come on, Simon." Edith Charles said.

She toed Simon Charles in the back but he was unresponsive.

"That is five bullets you have used." I said. The barrel of the gun turned to point at me. I tried to sound brave but my voice quavered slightly as I continued. "One bullet left. You can only shoot once more. Your husband is dead. There is nowhere to escape. Put the gun down and we can talk about it."

Edith Charles shook her head. Panic flooded her face and, for a moment, I was afraid she would shoot me. Then her face cleared.

"Simon?"

The plaintive sound of her voice tore at me. I have always been a sucker for pretty girls. I took a slow step forward.

Edith Charles turned and bolted from the room.

I immediately darted to Bakerson's side. The doctor joined me a moment later and checked for a pulse.

"I'm sorry." Doctor Peters got up and moved to Simon Charles.

I closed my eyes for a moment in a silent prayer. I felt someone pat me on the shoulder and looked up to see Kurt Heiss.

"He looks surprised." Kurt said.

He was right. Rather than pain or anger Bakerson's brutish face was relaxed and tranquil. His piggish eyes were open in surprise. He looked almost handsome in an ugly way.

I felt a momentary twang of regret. I had not treated him with respect. Instead I had automatically assumed his guilt.

"Simon Charles is still alive."

The doctor's surprised voice pulled me from my stupor. I crossed quickly to his side.

"The knife has severed a major blood vessel in his stomach. I fear that he will not live long." Doctor Peters said.

"Let me talk to him." I said. I elbowed the doctor aside.

"Should you not be chasing after her?" Lord Vellance asked.

"Where can she run to?"

I shook Simon Charles by the arm and, when he did not respond, placed my hand on his stomach and pressed. He woke with a scream.

"Who hired you?" I demanded.

"What the devil are you doing?"

The doctor grabbed me and tried to drag me away from his patient. I shrugged him off. I cannot say I am proud of the next few moments but I was desperate for information.

I pressed harder.

"Who hired you?"

"The Magister," screamed Simon Charles.

He collapsed unconscious from the pain.

I stood up, conscious of the accusing eyes looking at me. My right hand was dripping with the blood of a killer.

"She still has your gun." Kurt Heiss said. "We need to catch her."

I nodded and, avoiding the silent stares, opened the door and peered out. The corridor was empty and, what I could see of the dining room, that was empty also. Rodders, the steward, was standing at the head of the stairs to the bedroom wing. He pointed towards the kitchen.

"She went that way."

The cook in the kitchen pointed to the hatch in the ceiling.

"She had a gun and told us not to follow." The cook explained.

I motioned to her to stay and climbed the ladder. The hatch was open and I peered up into the pantry. It was very dark. I felt around for the clockwork light. It was missing.

I was very conscious that I was silhouetted against the hatch. Edith Charles would have the perfect opportunity to shoot me. But no shot rang out. I had the sudden urge to urinate. It felt like the worst of my night terrors. A darkened room. A killer with nothing to lose. I was weaponless.

I jumped slightly as Kurt Heiss grabbed my shoulder. He had climbed through the hatch after me and into the pantry. I formed a fist with my hands and tried to control their trembling.

"Is she here?"

I bit off a sharp reply and replied to the negative. The pantry was cold but I could feel a warm breeze to my right.

"Ask the steward for a clockwork light and we can start searching." I said. I tried to sound confident.

While Kurt spoke to the steward, I moved to the right. As I suspected, Edith Charles had untied the canvas separating the pantry from the rest of the balloon. There was a warm breeze from that direction.

I climbed through the small hole and stood on a metal gantry. I could feel vibrations through the soles of my feet. Someone was moving along the gantry. I stepped forward, my hands questing and found the railing.

A light stabbed behind me.

Someone had issued Kurt with a torch. He climbed through the tear in the canvas and joined me on the gantry. He shone the torch towards the bow of the balloon, then back towards the stern.

"Should we go forward or back towards the stern?"

I thought for a moment. The wheelhouse of the airship was towards the front. If she went forward, she would be more likely to meet a member of the crew.

"Towards the stern." I said. "Let the captain deal with the front."

I waited as Kurt relayed my comments to the steward.

The gantry trembled at each step I took. The light darted to the left and right at each intersection, checking for intruders. There was no one there.

I could feel the panic rising inside me as we quested forward in the dark. The sacs of helium loomed out of the darkness casting monstrous shadows that jumped ahead of us.

The airship was huge.

We seemed to be walking forever when I heard a slight sound ahead. I shushed Kurt and listened carefully. The sound repeated itself. It was a slight scuff of shoes on the metal gantry. Someone was just ahead of us.

I froze.

Kurt pointed the torch towards the distant stern and we waited. A shadow detached itself from the gloom, shuffling towards us. It was a member of the crew.

"Have you seen anyone up here?" I asked.

We were standing in a huge dome surrounded by cathedral sized helium sacs. I expected my voice to echo in this cathedral like space. Instead my voice sounded strange, a higher pitch than normal.

The crew member came forward into the light. He was dressed in a stoker's uniform, his grey blouse stained black by coke from the steam engine. His face was black except where the goggles had protected his eyes.

"The captain sent a message on the blower asking us to check up 'ere sir." He said with a gravelly voice. "I've seen nothing from the engine room forward. Johnson, he's another crew member, he's checking further aft sir."

The crew member turned and started to shuffle towards the stern. I followed him for a moment then, impatient by his slow pace, brushed past him with an apology. Kurt followed, holding the light steady.

We continued to check left and right at the intersections before proceeding forward. I was moving with less caution now that I knew other crew members were up here.

"There."

Kurt's whisper roused me. The darkness, the silence, the intense fear, together they had conspired to allow my brain to wander.

I could see a glow ahead. It was pointing at something on the floor of the gantry. We moved forward. I insisted that Kurt continually checks each intersection in case this was a distraction.

It wasn't.

Johnson was holding a torch. He pointed at my revolver which lay on the gantry floor. I stopped him from picking it up. I knelt down and used a clean handkerchief to lift it.

"Evidence." I whispered. I cracked open the cylinder and confirmed that there was one bullet left. "She must have dropped it in her hurry."

"Have you seen her?" Kurt asked.

"No sir." Johnson replied. "But there is an open inspection hatch at the stern of the balloon for inspecting the propeller."

Johnson led us towards the stern of the airship. A hatch lay open. A line fed through the winch and down into the blackness. I borrowed the torch from Johnson and pointed it into the depths below.

The propeller turned at a sedate pace pushing us forward towards London. I could feel each sweep of the massive blade churning the air. I could see the ground. Trees fled past, followed by a brief glint of river, then more trees. The rope dragged behind us, sometimes touching the tops of trees as it played catchup.

"Winch the rope in." I said.

I watched as Johnson expertly spun the winch, winding the rope up into a huge reel. It only took a few moments before the rope was wound in and the hatch closed.

"Look here."

Kurt pointed at a tiny piece of torn cloth that had caught on a nail. He pulled it loose and handed it to me. In the light of the torch I could see it was green silk, the same colour as the dress Edith Charles had worn.

"Let us return to the wheelhouse." I said. "If we are quick enough we can send a radio telegram ahead and request a search party to this location. I cannot imagine that she will get far in the dark."

In truth, I did not believe she survived a climb from that height.

Chapter Thirty-Three

The return to London was uneventful.

We crowded the deck as the crew returned the Airship Arcadia to her berth. There was no fanfare, no press waiting to receive us as we disembarked the hastily rolled out gangplank. A single ambulance waited. The ambulance crew had a last minute cigarette. There was no rush. Simon Charles had died in his sleep.

I waited on deck for the other passengers to leave. The captain had sent a radio telegram ahead and made hotel reservations for each of us. Cabs thronged the parking area, their chimneys puffed clouds of steam into the frigid morning air. I could see the police inspector waiting patiently at the back.

Mr and Mrs Potts shook my hand and thanked me. The ambulance crews got excited for a moment when they say her blood-stained bandages.

Lord and Lady Vellance disembarked next. Horace Vellance ignored me. His head held high, he marched down the gangplank. Lady Vellance cast me a hurried 'thank you'.

"Those two are a pair." Elisabeth said.

"I'm noticed you waited until your Aunt Imogen was distracted before you made that comment." I glanced over to Imogen who talked in an animated fashion with Mrs Colchester.

Elisabeth's eyes were bright with mischief.

"Well Ignatius Brown, it was a pleasure to make your acquaintance."

I shook Kurt's hand. He was in a hurry to return to Germany and was already booked on the next airship.

We all stood in silence as each of the bodies were removed from the airship. Several police officers acted as pallbearers. Elisabeth clutched my hand as Mrs Fabersham's body was carried down.

Mr Herts's body was last. Roland Ashton followed it down without looking at either of us. A man in a naval uniform met him at the foot of the gangplank and led him off.

Mrs Colchester made her goodbyes, giving Elisabeth her card. "She has invited us for tea." Elisabeth later told me when I asked. Apparently I was not invited.

I shook hands with Kurt and Dorothy again, and waved to them as they left.

"I would like to introduce you to someone." I said.

I led the way down the gangplank carrying my valise. The stewards followed last, carrying our trunks. I limped across the platform towards the dwindling cabs. The inspector was waiting for me.

"Ladies, this is Inspector Hopkins of Scotland Yard." I said. "Inspector Hopkins, this is my cousin Lady Imogen LaRue and my second cousin once removed Miss Elisabeth Murphy."

I waited for them to shake hands before opening my valise. I removed my book, the Biography of Dr John H. Watson, and handed it to Inspector Hopkins.

"These are the stolen plans." I said. "I swapped the real papers for the biography. I left the outer covers the same. I knew that the killer would find it hard to resist to steal it. I did not want to risk the real papers."

"Very well done." Inspector Hopkins said. "We will return them to their rightful owners at the admiralty. You should be very proud of your cousin, Lady LaRue."

"I am." Imogen said and gave my arm an affectionate shake.

"I am too." Elisabeth said, her eyes shining.

"Unfortunately I will have to cut your holiday short Ignatius." The Inspector said. "There has been a murder and we need someone with your experience to take charge of the case."

"Yes sir." I said. "It will be good to get back."

My leg hurt abominably. I was exhausted. My heart was sick from the murders.

But I was alive, and the Magister was out there.

The End

Printed in Great Britain
by Amazon